Slocum stared toward the horsemen slowly nearing the hill. "The one out front's called Half Eye by the Apache. Scar by the white man. If they decide to come after us, we'll be going up against the best mounted infantry troops who ever cocked a carbine."

The chill along Jimmy's spine went colder despite the scorching sun overhead. His heart pounded rapidly against his ribs. He peered through the shimmering heat waves; a dust devil danced through the prickly pear and ocotillo in the shadow valley. He didn't see the Indians. They had dropped from view behind a low swell in a bend of the creek three hundred yards away. The shadow from the stunted mesquites had lengthened noticeably, and still the Indians didn't appear. Relief surged through Jimmy's cramping gut.

"Looks like they've turned off, Slocum."

Slocum thumbed the hammer of his Winchester to full cock. "Hate to spoil your hopes, Jimmy. Remember what I said. Don't waste any ammunition. Make sure you have a clear target before you touch off a round."

Jimmy's heart skidded into his belly. Even as Slocum spoke, Jimmy spotted a quick flash of movement behind a greasewood clump just over a hundred yards downslope. "Slocum, I sure wish just once you could be wrong," Jimmy said, his voice shaky.

The Apaches were coming. . . .

DON'T MISS THESE
ALL-ACTION WESTERN SERIES
FROM THE BERKLEY PUBLISHING GROUP

THE GUNSMITH by J. R. Roberts
Clint Adams was a legend among lawmen, outlaws, and ladies. They called him . . . the Gunsmith.

LONGARM by Tabor Evans
The popular long-running series about U.S. Deputy Marshal Long—his life, his loves, his fight for justice.

SLOCUM by Jake Logan
Today's longest-running action Western. John Slocum rides a deadly trail of hot blood and cold steel.

BUSHWHACKERS by B. J. Lanagan
An action-packed series by the creators of Longarm! The rousing adventures of the most brutal gang of cutthroats ever assembled—Quantrill's Raiders.

JAKE LOGAN

SLOCUM AND THE SHOWDOWN AT SHILOH

J

JOVE BOOKS, NEW YORK

SHOWDOWN AT SHILOH

A Jove Book / published by arrangement with
the author

PRINTING HISTORY
Jove edition / October 1999

All rights reserved.
Copyright © 1999 by Penguin Putnam Inc.
This book may not be reproduced in whole or in part,
by mimeograph or any other means, without permission.
For information address: The Berkley Publishing Group,
a division of Penguin Putnam Inc.,
375 Hudson Street, New York, New York 10014.

The Penguin Putnam Inc. World Wide Web site address is
http://www.penguinputnam.com

ISBN: 0-515-12659-4

A JOVE BOOK®
Jove Books are published by The Berkley Publishing Group,
a division of Penguin Putnam Inc.,
375 Hudson Street, New York, New York 10014.
JOVE and the "J" design
are trademarks belonging to Penguin Putnam Inc.

PRINTED IN THE UNITED STATES OF AMERICA

10 9 8 7 6 5 4 3 2 1

1

The big bay between Slocum's knees sensed trouble several heartbeats before Slocum did.

The half-Morgan gelding stopped almost in mid-stride. His head came up, ears pointed straight ahead. The horse's nostrils fluttered a soft warning; a slight but distinct quiver rippled the skin along the bay's muscled neck.

Slocum's hand dropped to the stock of the rifle in its saddle sheath beside his right knee. In this country, a man paid attention when his horse went on the alert—or else he rode into a trap. The bay knew what he was doing.

The scent reached Slocum's nostrils then. The faint smell of woodsmoke and broiling meat drifted on the light breeze that blew into Slocum's face. A campfire on this narrow tributary of the Beaver River meant a man, or men. And most men in this rugged country were the kind who would drop a hammer first, then look to see who they had shot.

Slocum mentally cursed himself for his lapse of attention. That he had seen no trace of a living soul for the last three days was no excuse. Mistakes like that could get a man dead.

He unsheathed the rifle, cracked the action to make sure a cartridge was chambered, thumbed back the hammer, and kneed the bay into a slow, cautious walk along the narrow arroyo. The arroyo was little more than a deep draw carved by wind and weather and the shallow trickle of spring-fed

1

water that twisted along the sandy bottom on its way to the Beaver River a half mile to the south.

Slocum's gaze swept the walls of the arroyo, studded with sandstone rocks and wind-stunted cedars, as he rode. He saw nothing move, heard nothing. But nothing didn't build a campfire in the middle of nowhere. The hairs prickled on Slocum's forearms. The sensation of being watched grew with each slow stride of the bay gelding.

The horse's nostrils fluttered again as he rounded a sharp bend in the arroyo. A few yards ahead, near the edge of the shallow stream, a few small sticks of driftwood smoldered. On a sharpened, crooked stick propped across the fire on forked limbs, the skinned carcass of a rabbit dripped juices into the coals below. There was no sign of cooking utensils other than a blackened tin can beside the fire. A single frayed gray blanket, rolled into an uneven bundle and tied with twine, lay a few feet away from the smoldering blaze. Beside the blanket rested a gallon jug, a leather thong tied around the neck.

There was no sign of human life.

But no man just walked off and left his supper—

"Hold it right there, mister!"

Slocum stiffened at the call. It came from behind and a bit to his right. "Put that gun away or I'll shoot you sure enough dead!" The voice cracked a bit on the last word. Slocum made no move to turn; he knew where the voice had come from. He had ridden past the rocky outcrop less than a minute ago and had heard, smelled, or seen nothing. He cursed his carelessness again. A man who let himself be flanked, never sensed the presence of a bushwhacker, had no one to blame but himself if he caught a slug in the back.

Slocum lowered the hammer of the rifle and slid the Winchester back into its scabbard. A cold spot seemed to form between his shoulder blades, more from his lingering anger at himself than from any real fear of death.

"All right, mister! Now lift your hands! Don't turn around, or I'll drop you!"

Slocum couldn't tell from the tenor of the words whether the speaker was a young boy, a girl, or a grown man with a voice that had never fully matured.

Whoever it was had him dead to rights, and knew it.

Moments later, the bay gelding half turned his head, the right ear cocked, listening. Slocum heard the whisper of footsteps on sand behind him, the steps those of someone light on their feet. The footfalls stopped for several heartbeats.

Slocum had the bushwhacker's position now—behind his right shoulder. He might—just might—be able to draw the Colt revolver he wore cross-draw style on his left hip, twist in the saddle, and fire. The odds were thin. Slocum was fast with a handgun, but no man was fast enough to get off a round before someone holding a cocked weapon could pull a trigger. It would be a last-ditch, desperation gamble, if it came to that. And he knew he'd probably catch some lead in the process.

"You ain't one of 'em." The voice was within a few feet now.

"Whoever *they* are, I'm not," Slocum said, his tone steady and calm.

"All right, you can turn around now. But don't try nothin' funny, or I swear I'll shoot you."

Slocum slowly reined the bay around.

The small black bore of a .22-caliber Remington single-shot rifle pointed straight at the second button on Slocum's chest. The head resting on the stock of the little rifle was mostly a mop of long, sandy, and tangled hair rippling in the breeze.

The face behind the sights belonged to a kid.

But it didn't take a grown man to pull a trigger, and Slocum knew the puny .22 slug could be as deadly as a canister shell from a six-pounder cannon. The difference was that, unless the little lead pill hit heart or brain, a man was a lot longer dying than he would be from a cannon ball.

"Easy now," Slocum said softly. "I mean you no harm. Lower the gun and we'll talk."

Indecision flickered for an instant in the brown eyes behind the rifle sights. "Maybe you ain't one of 'em, but how do I know I can trust you?"

"You don't," Slocum said.

The rifle barrel dropped. The full face now visible was sunburned and peeling, cheeks thin to the point of being gaunt. The boy's clothing was little more than rags, elbows and knees poking through holes in a faded, handmade shirt and bib over-alls. A smear of blood showed at the tops of used-up brogans where the leather had bit into sockless ankles. The youth's toes protruded from holes in both shoes.

Slocum nodded casually toward the rifle. "Might want to lower the hammer of the long gun," he said. "The muzzle's pointed toward your foot. If the hammer happened to drop, you'd have a hole in your instep."

The boy glanced at the weapon, seemed to blush—it was hard to tell beneath the sunburn—and immediately shifted the rifle aside and lowered the hammer.

"Reckon I got careless there for a minute."

"We both did. Man can get hurt doing that."

The youth stared at Slocum for a moment, a touch of defiance mixed with curiosity in his light hazel eyes. "How come you didn't laugh at me?"

"I never laugh at a man who's holding a gun. Especially when it's pointed at me." Slocum canted his head over his shoulder. "Your supper's going to burn."

Indecision flickered in the boy's eyes. "How do I know you won't jump me when I let my guard down?"

"You don't. For what it's worth, though, I'll give you my word. One man to another."

The youth studied Slocum for a moment, then nodded. "I reckon I can trust you. I ain't got much. Just that one skinny rabbit. You're welcome to share, if you're hungry."

"I'd appreciate that," Slocum said with a solemn nod. "Maybe I can stir up something to go along with the rabbit. Which one of us is going to lead the way to the camp?"

"I said I'd trust you." The boy strode past Slocum's bay, limping slightly. He moved a bit like a tired old man, shoulders slumped, heels dragging. But Slocum knew the kid could move like an Apache when he wanted to. Or Slocum wouldn't have been so easily surprised.

Slocum dismounted, loosened the cinches, and hitched his bay to a stunted juniper a few feet from the fire. He lifted the canvas possibles sack from its tie-down across his saddlebags, and carried it to the fire as the youngster moved the stick with the blackened rabbit carcass from above the remnants of the small fire and stared at it in disgust.

"May be burnt too much to eat," the boy said.

"Don't fret it. I'll stir up something."

As he worked, Slocum casually surveyed the campsite. It didn't take much study. One fire, one burned rabbit, one dirty, torn blanket, and one ragamuffin youngster.

Neither spoke as Slocum fixed what passed for average trail camp fare—thick slabs of bacon, water gravy, coffee, some biscuits left over from yesterday's camp, and a tin of beans heated in the can. He purposely cooked enough to feed three men. If he was any judge, the kid hadn't eaten much in a spell.

Slocum carried only one tin plate, and the boy obviously had none. It wasn't a problem. He filled the plate for himself; the boy ate from the skillet. The kid tried hard to pace himself, but after a few bites gave up the pretense and shoveled the grub in like a field hand, using the blunt blade of a worn pocket knife for a fork and sopping up the last of the grease with part of a biscuit—his fourth.

When the last bite was gone, the boy finally looked up from the skillet, sighed, and sipped coffee from a battered tin can he carried rolled in his worn blanket. The dented, scorched tin was the kid's only camp equipment, Slocum figured.

"Much obliged, mister," he said. "Mighty fine eatin'."

"My pleasure, friend." Slocum sipped at his coffee, then pulled a thin Mexican cheroot from his pocket and fired the smoke with a sulphur-tipped match.

There was no discussion of who would clean up Slocum's utensils. The kid rose and carried everything but the coffeepot, his tin can, and Slocum's cup to a shallow pool in the creek. He scrubbed the utensils with sand, rinsed them, and handed them back to Slocum. The way the boy had slicked the skillet with those biscuits, Slocum wasn't sure the fry pan had needed scrubbing all that much.

The two sat for a moment in silence, Slocum working the cheroot, the boy sitting at his side, staring into the fading coals of the campfire. Finally, the youth looked up at Slocum.

"I know it ain't polite to butt into a man's business, mister, but can I ask something?"

"Ask away. If you'll let me ask a question or two later. And neither of us has to answer if we don't want to."

"Fair enough. What's your name?"

"Slocum."

"James Daniel Forrest. Most folks call me Jimmy." The boy stuck out a hand. Slocum took it. The calluses at the base of the fingers and across the heel of the palm seemed out of place on one so young. The grip was firmer than Slocum expected.

"Pleasure to meet you, Jimmy," Slocum said.

"Where you headed?"

Slocum shrugged. From a grown man, he wouldn't have bothered answering the question, because it was nobody's business. But for some reason Slocum couldn't fully explain, he found himself taking a liking to the ragged kid who had appeared in the middle of nowhere. Maybe, he thought, it was because the boy had guts enough to take on a grown man—and was savvy enough to make sure he had the edge when he did.

"No place in particular, Jimmy. Just passing through. You?"

"Trackin' some men." Jimmy's face twisted. Slocum couldn't tell if the boy's expression reflected bitterness, hurt, or rage.

"Alone and on foot? I didn't see a horse around," Slocum said. He lifted a hand. "Mind you, if you don't want to talk about it, that's all right. It's none of my business."

Jimmy fell silent for a moment, studying Slocum, then nodded. "Reckon it wouldn't hurt to talk on it. Like I said, I'm trackin' some men. I ain't got a horse. Had one, but them men took him, along with our others."

The reference to "our" piqued Slocum's interest, but he didn't push the point. Jimmy would tell the whole story when, and if, he decided to tell it; until then, it was the boy's business, and his alone.

"These men—are they the ones you said back up the trail I wasn't one of?" Slocum asked.

"Yes, sir."

"Just call me Slocum, Jimmy. No need to add a 'sir' to it. How'd you know I wasn't one of them?"

"Your horse's tracks didn't match them I been followin'."

"If they had?"

"I'd have shot you. In the back."

Slocum nodded. "The safest and most efficient way to get rid of an enemy." He lifted an eyebrow. "When you find those men, what do you plan to do?"

"Get my sister back. And kill 'em all. Every last one," Jimmy said in a flat, emotionless tone. The boy's gaze settled on the Colt at Slocum's left hip. "You in the war, Mr. Slocum?"

"More than I wanted to be."

"Cavalry?"

"What makes you think that?"

"Dad wears"—Jimmy's voice broke for an instant—"wore his side arm like that. Cross-draw. He was cavalry. He didn't talk much about the war."

"A lot of men don't, Jimmy. The ones who do generally weren't in the fighting and aren't worth listening to."

Slocum finished his cheroot, ground the butt into the sand beneath a heel, and studied the young man's face for a moment. The shift in tense from "wears" to "wore" when Jimmy spoke of his father, the mention of a sister, the references to the men he tracked said a lot. And even though it was none of his concern, Slocum's instincts told him the sunburned, tattered young man wanted—needed—to talk.

"What happened, Jimmy? From the beginning," Slocum said gently.

The boy sighed, stared off into the distance, and finally nodded.

"We—my dad, mom, sissy, and me—had us a little ranch up on the Republican. Wasn't much, but we was happy enough there." Slocum thought he saw a hint of moisture in the boy's eyes, as if he were about to cry but determined not to.

"Them men—six of 'em, best I can tell from the tracks—come by. Killed Dad and—" his voice caught for a moment—"did things to Mom. Then killed her too. They burned the house and barn, took Sissy, and run off all our horses and cows." Jimmy's gaze locked on Slocum's. "I was off huntin' a couple miles away when it happened. Time I seen the smoke and run home, it was too late. If I'd been there, maybe . . ." His voice trailed away, pushed down by the weight of unspoken but obvious guilt.

"They probably would have killed you too, Jimmy," Slocum said. "You said your place was on the Republican. Is that the river by that name up in Nebraska?"

Jimmy nodded silently.

Slocum's brows lifted in wonder. The Republican River was a couple hundred miles to the north. "So you walked all the way, tracking the men?"

"Didn't see no other way."

"Couldn't you have gone for help? A neighbor maybe, or the law?"

The boy was silent for a moment. "Maybe I could have. But it was so far. Forty miles to the nearest neighbor, old Mr. Groensfeld's place, and he wouldn't of been no help. And the law—well, the closest lawman to us was near a hundred miles off, and drunk most of the time. Never left his own county anyway. Seemed to me it'd be a waste of time. So I gathered up what I could, which wasn't much on account of they burned the house, and lit out after them."

"But on foot," Slocum said. "You could have borrowed or stolen a horse."

Jimmy shook his head. "Wouldn't have been right, even if there'd been one around. Dad always said it wasn't right to steal. Didn't stop them men." His tone tightened a bit. "But they made a mistake, Mr. Slocum. They didn't hunt me down and kill me."

Slocum nodded silently. There was no questioning Jimmy's tone, or the set of the young, beardless jaw. The kid was determined. He'd either find those men or die along the way. Most likely the latter, Slocum figured. Starvation, thirst, a rattler, break a leg in a fall, stumble onto an outlaw camp or a prowling band of reservation-jumping Indians. There were hundreds of ways to die in this country. Most of them unpleasant.

"So you've been on the trail since then, with no food or supplies?" Slocum asked.

Jimmy patted the scarred stock of the old Remington .22 single-shot. "I got my rifle. It'll feed me as long as I got ammunition." The boy fell silent for a moment. Slocum let Jimmy work his way through his own thoughts long enough to start another pot of coffee. He lit a second cheroot and squatted on his heels at the boy's side.

"True enough, a man can live off the land if he's a good enough shot," Slocum finally said. "Jimmy, you know you can't catch up with them if they're on horseback and you're afoot."

"I'll catch 'em. Mr. Slocum. I got my whole life to get that done. Sooner or later, they'll stop, and I'll find 'em. I'll get Sissy back, and then I'll kill 'em."

Slocum silently questioned the boy's determination, but his admiration for the kid's grit grew. The boy didn't have the chance of a snowball in Hell, but he was going to do his damnedest. It was more than most men would have the guts to try.

Jimmy rose and reached for his rifle. "Time's wastin'. I gotta find their trail again. Lost it three days back after it stormed."

Slocum rubbed his chin, and winced at the scratch of palm against stubble. Jimmy wasn't the only one with a problem now. Slocum knew he couldn't just let the boy walk off into the night and almost certain death. The sense of responsibility fired a coal of resentment. He hadn't asked for this. But then, he wasn't going anyplace that couldn't wait a few days. The Grand Teton Mountains and Jackson Hole would still be in Wyoming after he knew the boy was safe and in good hands. If he'd been dealing with a man grown, Slocum wouldn't hesitate to ride on. This was different. This was just a kid.

"Hold up a minute, Jimmy," Slocum said, glancing at the shadows creeping toward the east side of the camp. "It'll be dark in a couple of hours. Why don't we just camp here for the night, get some rest? There's good water here. It's a long way to the next spring, if you're headed south or west." He nodded toward the boy's bleeding ankles. "Maybe I can patch those shoes up some, so they won't hurt your feet so much."

The boy hesitated, sunburned forehead wrinkled in thought, then nodded. "Reckon you got a point. Won't be a moon tonight. Might walk across their tracks and miss 'em in the dark." He sat back down, put the .22 at his side, and studied Slocum. "Like I said, I reckon I can trust you. Anyhow, I got nothin' worth stealin'." After a moment, he said, "Mr. Slocum, I sure enough hate to ask, but have you got any of them biscuits left?"

Slocum suppressed a smile. Most half-starved boys wouldn't have hesitated to ask. "Might be a couple." He took two from the possibles sack and handed them to Jimmy.

"Sure this won't throw you short?" the boy asked.

"Not at all, Jimmy. I fitted out pretty well before I left Clarksville."

The boy finished the last biscuit, and licked a crumb from his chapped lower lip. "Where's that?"

"East and a touch south of here, on the Red River."

"That your home, Mr. Slocum?"

"No. Just went there to take care of some business. And visit a friend."

"Where is your home?"

Slocum sighed softly. "No place in particular, Jimmy. Just wherever I happened to be at the time."

The boy unrolled his single, worn blanket. Slocum noticed the cloth was thin, riddled with holes. "Man ought to have a home, Mr. Slocum. A place where he can raise a few cattle, some horses maybe." Before Slocum could reply, the youngster added, "Forget I said that. Ain't none of my business. Sometimes when I get real tired, I talk way too much. Even when there ain't nobody around to talk to."

"It's all right, Jimmy. And you're right. Most men need a place to call home." Slocum heard the hint of wistfulness in his own words. He had known only one home. One that he'd left on the run years ago and could never see again, even if he truly wanted to.

Jimmy removed his worn, bloodied shoes and stretched out on the blanket.

"Toss your shoes over here," Slocum said. "I'll see what I can do to fix them up enough to at least keep the cactus out of your toes." He caught the shoes Jimmy tossed one at a time, studied them for a moment, and shook his head silently. There wasn't much he could do, but he'd do the best he could with what he had to work with. He reached into a saddlebag for his tools and the spare leather and thongs he carried for emergency equipment repairs.

The light was fading fast now. When the sun went down in this country, it didn't waste time about it—just crashed into and under the western horizon. Slocum stoked the fire, partly for light to work by, partly for warmth. Even in late spring, the nights turned chilly in the Beaver River country. He thought for a moment about offering Jimmy his spare blanket, then decided against it. The boy might take offense, and Slocum didn't want to hurt his feelings. From what he'd picked up in the conversations so far, young James Daniel Forrest had been hurt enough in the last few weeks.

He went to work on the shoes.

"Mr. Slocum?"

The young man's voice, already on the edge of sleep, was barely audible over the chirp of crickets and distant chorus of coyotes beginning their night songs.

"Yes?"

"I never been this far south. You?"

"I've been over most of the West at one time or another."

"What's the country like? Say between here and Mexico?"

Slocum glanced up from his work. Jimmy had propped himself up on one elbow, the expression on his face completely open and trusting.

"It's mostly big and empty, Jimmy. A man could get lost easily if he wanders away from the roads and towns, and there's not many road and towns. For the most part, it's dry— a long way between watering holes. You think the men you're after are headed for Mexico?" He bent back over the shoes, stitching a soft elkskin patch over the outer third of a vamp.

The boy's eyes narrowed. "That's my guess. Tracks have been headin' mostly south by southwest all the way from Nebraska. I hear outlaws like Mexico."

"It depends," Slocum said. "If he's not wanted south of the Rio Grande, Mexico is reasonably safe for a man on the run. American lawmen have no jurisdiction there."

"What's juries—jurisdiction?"

"Authority. It means they don't have the right to legally cross the border and arrest anybody, white or brown, in Mexico."

"How about somebody who ain't the law? They got any of that jurisdiction there?"

Slocum shrugged. "A man's pretty much on his own down there to go where he pleases, as long as he doesn't offend anybody. Some Mexicans don't like Anglos like us much. Most of them are easygoing people, not at all hard to get along with if you don't break their laws and make sure you observe their customs."

The boy settled back onto his blanket and lay staring at the stars. "Then I'll be nice and polite to the Mexicans. I just want to get Sissy back before I kill them men."

Slocum trimmed a thick strip of leather into a crude moccasin-type sole and reached for his awl. "Sissy's real important to you, isn't she?"

"She's all the family I got left. Even before—before them men came, we was best friends. Ever since I can remember."

"What's she like?"

Jimmy's throat seemed to tighten. "She's—nice, I reckon, would be a good way to say it. Aw, we fuss some, like most brothers and sisters, but when I got somethin' troublin' me, she's the one I go talk to." The boy sighed. "She's pretty, Mr. Slocum. Long blond hair and blue eyes. But she's real old—not near as old as you, but old. Nineteen, I think, maybe twenty."

Slocum stifled a grin. He'd been called a lot of things in his life, but not often "old." But to somebody Jimmy's age, Slocum supposed, he would seem ancient. He finished with the awl, threaded a heavy-gauge harness needle with beeswax-coated saddle stitching, and started sewing the new leather sole into place. "Mind if I ask how old you are, Jimmy?"

"Fifteen."

Slocum glanced up again, an eyebrow raised.

Jimmy lowered his gaze. "Well, almost. My next birthday anyway. Come November."

Fourteen years old, Slocum thought with a touch of bitterness. An age when a boy should be spending his time hunting and fishing and doing his reading and numbers, not trying to single-handedly track down and kill six tough, grown men.

Slocum wasn't sure what to say next, but Jimmy solved the problem for him. The boy's head had dropped onto the blanket, his breathing regular and deep, and he was sound asleep.

Slocum finished with the second shoe as the boy slept; it was slow going by firelight, but he was satisfied he had done his best. He unrolled his own bedroll, pulled off his boots and hat, and stretched out, gunbelt at his side and the rifle within easy reach, and stared at the near-blanket of stars against the deep black sky overhead.

He wasn't sure what to do next, and that aggravated him. Slocum wasn't used to that feeling of indecision.

But one thing was for certain. He couldn't ride away tomorrow and leave a fourteen-year-old boy alone in the middle of nowhere. He'd have to go with young James Daniel Forrest, at least until he was sure the boy would be all right.

After that, he'd rein the bay toward Jackson Hole.

A few days wouldn't matter to him.

They might mean a big difference for the boy.

2

Slocum awoke early, the stars still bright pinpoints of light in the black velvet canopy of sky.

Even if he weren't a light sleeper, Slocum still would have climbed from his blankets in the predawn hours. It was more than a long habit; this was his favorite time of day: the gradual change from starlight or moonlight to the faint, pale gray wash of predawn, then the first stirrings of animal life as the night prowlers went home and the day creatures went to work. The time of day when the land was at peace.

He glanced at the small form huddled in the single blanket a few feet away. Jimmy's breathing was deep and regular. He was wrapped in escape from the reality of a world of loss.

Twice during the night, Slocum had awakened.

Once, a faint scuffle along the sandy creek bed brought him alert, hand on the grips of the .44-40 revolver at his side. The weapon wasn't needed. Slocum relaxed and watched the raccoon dutifully wash its morsel of food in the narrow ribbon of water a few yards downstream.

The second time, a stifled half-cough, half-sob brought him awake. Jimmy's eyes were closed, but starlight glinted from the wetness on his cheeks.

Slocum left him alone.

Sometimes a man needed to cry, to let some of the pain out, even if it soon came back. Slocum knew it would embarrass Jimmy to be wakened, so he closed his eyes and drifted off to sleep again.

Now he slipped from his blankets. Moving quietly so as not to wake the boy, he started a small fire and made coffee. He squatted beside the blaze, lit a smoke, and listened, content, to the yelps and howls of coyotes, the lazy hoot of an owl returning to its favorite tree after a night's hunt, the stirring of small feet as the little creatures of the night went about their business along the stream.

The pale wash of false dawn gave way to one of those spectacular Plains sunrises of which Slocum never tired. The gray eastern horizon painted itself slowly, gray giving way to swatches of gold, orange, and red, all framed against shades of blue ranging from the color of cornflowers in the east to near-purple overhead.

"Mr. Slocum?"

The voice pulled his gaze from the color-splash of the dawn.

"Morning, Jimmy. Sleep well?"

The boy sat up, his blanket still wrapped around his shoulders against the morning chill, and rubbed a knuckle across his eyes. "I reckon so. Must have been more wore down than I thought."

"Walking a couple hundred miles can do that to a man. Hungry?"

"I could eat a little, I guess."

Half an hour later, Slocum had to stifle a grin. Jimmy had put away more than a little grub; Slocum again had cooked enough for three men. The boy had accounted for two of those three, and once again sopped up the last of the bacon grease from the skillet with the last biscuit in the pack.

Jimmy finished off the last morsel, sighed in contentment, then looked sheepishly at Slocum. "It ain't right," he said.

"What isn't?"

"Eatin' up all your grub like this. I can pay some."

Slocum cut off the offer with a casual wave. "Don't worry about it, Jimmy. You're not going to run me short."

"But it don't seem right. I mean, a man ought to pay his own way."

"True enough, Jimmy, and a man usually does—" Slocum stopped in mid-sentence, an ear cocked, listening; a few feet away the tethered bay snuffled a soft warning.

"What is it?" the boy asked softly.

"Horses coming. Two of them. From just around the bend in the creek. Grab your rifle. Make sure it's loaded. Then get up on the arroyo wall. Make sure you have a clean field of fire and good cover. Don't shoot unless you have to. Could be they're just cowboys out hunting strays." It was a possibility, Slocum thought, but a slim one. The country along the Beaver River was more known for hardcase men than for cows.

The boy reached for the .22 and rose to his bare feet. "Think they're bandits?"

"Maybe, maybe not. Let's not take any chances one way or the other."

"What are you going to do?"

"Wait and see who they are."

Jimmy clambered up the wall of the arroyo; seconds later, only the thin tube of the little rifle showed from beneath a stunted juniper bush twenty yards from the camp.

Slocum rose and stood casually, thumbs hooked into his cartridge belt, and waited as the hoofbeats neared.

Two horsemen rounded the bend of the creek: a big, blocky rider on a rangy blue roan and a much smaller man astride a little tight-twisted sorrel.

Slocum didn't need a formal introduction to know what they were. They wore the outlaw stamp as if it were a painted sign. Both carried sheathed rifles and wore side arms. Both started visibly at seeing Slocum; the breeze had been at their backs, carrying away the scent of woodsmoke. The surprise faded quickly. Their hands dropped near the grips of their revolvers.

The man on the blue roan reined in a dozen yards away and squinted through his one good eye at Slocum. A jagged scar ran from beneath his hat brim down through the second, empty eye socket. The man seemed relaxed, muscles loose.

His partner, almost a head shorter and slight of build, looked to be little more than a kid not yet in his twenties, faint blond stubble barely visible on his receding chin. And he was tense, jaw muscles bunched, eyes narrowed, obviously tight as a cheap fiddle string. The smaller man reined his sorrel to Slocum's right. They had done this before. Spread out the targets so one man didn't stand a chance against two.

Slocum also knew he might—or might not—be able to take them both down. There was a chance he could stop some lead in the process. But he had an ace in the hole.

If Jimmy didn't panic or freeze up, and if he saw that Slocum's attention was on the big man, the boy would drop the hammer on the other rider. The little .22 slug might not stop the man, except with a head shot. But fire from an unexpected source tended to distract a man, even if the shot was a clean miss. That slight distraction could make the difference.

Slocum had to trust the kid. He had no other choice.

The big man, the relaxed one, was the more dangerous of the two. The younger one's nerves worked against him; a man whose muscles were tight lost a fraction of a second on the draw and tended to rush the first shot. The one-eyed rider had to go down first.

A relaxed calm settled over Slocum, the familiar loosening of muscles and acute clarity of sight and sound that preceded a fight. It had kept him alive before, even through the carnage of the war.

"Howdy," the one-eyed man said.

"Morning," Slocum replied calmly. "Coffee's about gone, but I can make some more."

The big man—Slocum judged him about six feet, thick through the shoulders and heavy of thigh—shook his head. "We done had coffee." The man's blocky, square-jawed face turned toward Slocum's big bay. It was more than a casual glance.

Then the one eye turned back toward Slocum. A crooked grin bared a space where two front teeth had been.

"Nice pony."

"I've had worse."

"Reckon I'll take him."

"He's not for sale."

"Wasn't offerin' to buy the horse, friend. What I said was, I'll take him."

Slocum said softly, "I don't think so."

The big man's head wagged slightly. "Give you one thing, hoss," he said. "You got balls like a Mexican stud. Reckon a horse is worth dyin' for?"

"The question is," Slocum said, "do *you* think so?"

The big man's right shoulder twitched. He was fast, but not as fast as he thought. Slocum's slug kicked a puff of dust from the rider's shirt pocket before the big man's handgun cleared leather. Slocum twisted toward the smaller rider. He didn't fight the muzzle jump of the Peacemaker; he thumbed the hammer at the top of the recoil—and knew he was going to be too late.

The smaller man's revolver was clear of leather, the bore swinging towards Slocum's belly. Slocum heard the faint splat of lead against flesh, the almost inaudible pop of a .22 rimfire. The *pistolero*'s muscles jumped in startled reflex. The muzzle of his handgun drifted to one side.

Slocum let his Colt's barrel settle into line, held the trigger back, and slipped his thumb from the hammer. The soft lead, 200-grain slug hammered into the rider's ribs, the impact twisting him in the saddle.

But the little man was tough and game. He stayed in the stirrups despite the sideways jump of the frightened sorrel, fighting to bring his own revolver back into play.

Slocum's second round ripped into the base of the man's throat, snapped his head forward, then back. The gunman dropped straight down, flopped onto his spooked mount, bounced free as the horse bolted, and hit the sandy creek soil face-down.

He didn't move. Slocum knew the man was dead before he fell, his spine shattered by the second bullet.

Slocum started to turn toward the bigger man, still in the saddle despite the heart shot; Slocum had seen men drilled through the heart run several yards and empty a six-gun before going down. The one-eyed rider had pulled his revolver and now raised the weapon toward Slocum.

Jimmy's .22 cracked again. The big man seemed to cock his head for an instant. The handgun dropped from slack fingers. The man's horse spun and spilled the rider onto his side.

Even from a dozen yards away, Slocum could see the small, dark, round hole just behind the now-sightless eye.

It had been a perfect head shot.

Slocum flipped open the loading gate of his Peacemaker, ejected the spent cartridges, and thumbed fresh rounds into the cylinder.

"Good work, Jimmy!" Slocum called over the fading echoes of the gunshots. "You can come on down now! It's over!"

Minutes later, the boy sidled cautiously to the edge of the camp, the little Remington still tucked against his shoulder. His face was pale beneath the sunburn. The muzzle of the rifle jiggled slightly in trembling hands.

"It's okay, Jimmy," Slocum said softly. "They're both dead. Fine shooting, amigo."

The tremble in Jimmy's fingers seemed to spread until his whole body quivered. A natural reaction, Slocum knew. A lot of men stayed calm under fire, then started shaking all over when the shooting stopped. He put a reassuring hand on Jimmy's shoulder. The boy seemed to be bordering on shock; he needed time to gather his wits. Which was just as well, for Slocum still had some work to do.

"Might as well sit down and relax," Slocum said. "I'll saddle my bay and bring back their horses."

The outlaw mounts hadn't bolted more than a quarter mile. A short time later Slocum rode back into camp, the blue roan and snorting, walleyed sorrel trailing behind his bay. Slocum found hobbles in the dead men's saddlebags, strapped them around the fetlocks of the captured horses, loosened the cinches on all three animals, and ground-hitched his bay.

Jimmy, his face beginning to regain some color, sat and stared at the two dead men as Slocum strode to his side. The boy's fingers still trembled a bit, Slocum noticed, but he seemed to be getting a handle on things.

Slocum paused to check the bodies. Jimmy's first .22 slug, fired from an angle, had taken the smaller rider in the chest muscle just in front of the arm. Not a killing shot with a little 28-grain lead pill, but enough of a surprise to have cost the slight man his life a second later when Slocum's heavier slugs hit him. Jimmy's second shot had drilled through the big man's temple into his brain. That one would have dropped a buffalo in its tracks, Slocum thought.

He strode to Jimmy's side. "You okay?"

"I—I guess so." The thin voice quavered a bit. "It's just that—well, I never shot nobody before. It—gives me a kind of funny feelin'."

Slocum lit a smoke and nodded solemnly. "I know the feeling, Jimmy. Any man worth his salt feels it too. There are some who don't. They aren't human."

The boy fell silent for a moment, then shifted his gaze from the dead man to Slocum. "Does it bother you, Mr. Slocum? Killin', I mean?"

"Most times. Sometimes more than others. For what it's worth, remember you didn't have a choice. If you hadn't shot, you and I could very well be the dead ones by now." He dragged at the smoke, let it trickle through his nostrils. "Think you're up to more killing, Jimmy? When you find those men you're after, I mean?"

The youngster's jawline firmed. "Yes, sir. I don't reckon it'll bother me near as much to pull the trigger on them." After a moment's silence, the boy said, "Mr. Slocum, you're a gun hawk, ain't you? A shooter?"

The question caught Slocum a bit by surprise. "A gun hawk? No, I wouldn't say that exactly." He didn't add that most people on the frontier would. A reputation like his was hard to ride down and impossible to ride away from. There was always someone who thought he was faster. Slocum didn't fool himself. He could meet that man who not only thought he was faster, but actually was, at any time, any place. And there were those who waited to settle an old score, the kind of men who'd shoot him in the back, given the chance. "Why do you ask?"

"Because I never seen anybody as fast with a six-gun as you. Didn't get a good look, just out of the corner of my eye, on account of I was watchin' that littler man, but I barely seen you draw. Just kind of a blur, then your gun went off. You could have took them both, easy."

Slocum tapped the ash from his smoke and shook his head. "No, Jimmy. I'm serious—if you hadn't shot that smaller man when you did, he would have put lead in me. The only thing as bad as coming in second in a gunfight is finishing in a tie. You pulled my bacon out of the fire for sure.''

The boy fell silent again, sunburned brow knit in thought. After a couple of minutes, he lifted his gaze to Slocum.

"Mr. Slocum, maybe I ain't too smart, but I'm smart enough to know I'm just a kid who's never been to Texas and don't know the country. And that there ain't but one of me and there's six of them men who killed my folks and took my sister. I was wonderin'. . . .'' His voice trailed away; a faint flush seemed to color his cheeks.

The boy was smarter than he thought he was, Slocum granted. He didn't let stubborn pride get in the way of how things really were. "Go on, Jimmy," he prompted softly.

"Well, I was thinkin' maybe I could hire you, if you'd be of a mind. To help me find them men and get Sissy back.''

Slocum lifted an eyebrow. "A manhunt, especially when you don't know who you're after or where they're headed and they've got a long head start on you, takes a lot of time. And money. You'll need supplies, equipment. That all considered, do you have the money to hire a guide? They don't come cheap.''

Jimmy's face brightened. "I got money, Mr. Slocum. Lots of it. Twenty whole dollars, earned it myself. Had it buried in a glass jar out by the barn when them men came. They didn't find it.''

Slocum held back a wry smile and nodded solemnly. "That's a lot of money, Jimmy." Which was true enough, for a youngster Jimmy's age. A fortune.

"What makes you think I won't just take your money and ride off?''

"Because you ain't no thief, Mr. Slocum. I don't know how I know that, exactly, but I do. You could ride off easy enough, and I sure wouldn't hold that against you, but you won't steal from me. Or anybody else.''

Slocum raised his opinion of the sunburned farm boy another notch. Jimmy had good instincts, and the confidence to trust them. That was more than could be said about many grown men Slocum had known.

"I won't ride off and leave you out here, Jimmy. You wouldn't stand a chance in Texas on your own—"

Jimmy lifted a hand. "There's somethin' else. Another reason I want to hire you. I been tryin' to put myself in your boots, like Dad always said about figurin' out where another man stood, how he was thinkin'. And if I was you, I'd stay with me just long enough to dump me in some town somewhere, then ride on. If I hire you, we got us a con—what do you call it?"

"Contract."

"Yeah. A contract. So you'd be bound by your word you'd stand by me, right?"

"Right." The kid was thinking way ahead, Slocum mused; a good sign. He might be fourteen and not pushing fifteen very hard, but he was older than his age between the ears.

"So, what do you say, Mr. Slocum?"

Slocum sighed. He hadn't planned on winding up nursemaiding a young kid through hundreds of miles of dangerous country on a cold trail, where any minute could be their last. But then, he had to admit, he liked this freckled-faced farm boy. Liked his grit and common sense. And Slocum wasn't going anyplace in particular that wouldn't keep.

"All I can promise, Jimmy, is that I'll help you as best I can. For your part, if we find out it's impossible—that we can't identify them, let alone find them—you'll give it up and make another life for yourself."

The boy frowned for a long time, studying on the proposal, then shook his head. "I can't let it drop, Mr. Slocum. Not until I at least get Sissy back. Or—or find out she's dead. Any time you think it ain't possible, you just say so and ride on, no hard feelin's. But I'll spend the rest of my life trackin' em if I have to, and I'll find 'em. Sooner or later. Or I'll die tryin'."

Slocum said, "That's what I wanted to hear. I don't ride with a man who gives up too easily. You've got a deal, Jimmy." He extended a hand. The boy took it eagerly and, Slocum sensed, with relief. The youth's hands seemed bigger than Slocum remembered. "One thing, though. If we're going to be riding together, drop the 'Mr.' Just call me Slocum."

"Yes, sir."

"We can do without the 'sir' too. Partners aren't all that formal on the trail."

"I'm pleased and proud to be your partner, Mr.—uh, Slocum." Jimmy released Slocum's hand, reached into a pocket, brought out a wad of crumpled greenbacks, and held them out.

Slocum shook his head. "Your word's good enough for me, Jimmy. I know I'll be paid when the job's done. Meantime, we've already got a few problems solved."

"What's that?"

Slocum nodded toward the hobbled blue roan, the sorrel, and the bodies. "We've got you a saddle and horse, a spare mount for a pack animal or riding, whatever camp gear and supplies these men were carrying, and any money they have on them. The smaller man's clothes might fit you well enough for now. And you might could use a bit more firepower than that .22."

"You mean, take their stuff? But—well, it ain't ours, Slocum. Would that be right?"

"They have no use for it any longer, do they?"

"I reckon not. Still, it don't seem right—"

"Would they have given us the same consideration, Jimmy? They chose the trail they rode. It just ended a little sooner than they expected."

The boy sighed. "If you look at it that way, you got a point. More like the spoils of war, as Dad used to say."

"Then let's see what we've got," Slocum said.

The inventory didn't take long; the two outlaws had been traveling light, as did most men on the dodge. And like most outlaws, they were almost broke. Between them, they had six dollars and change. But all in all, Slocum was pleased with the quick tally.

Slocum and Jimmy wouldn't have to share eating utensils, and the dead men had carried a good supply of camp fare in their possibles sack. The smaller man's saddle, a single-fire rig with a deep, comfortable seat and prominent swells to cradle the upper thighs in case a horse decided to pitch, needed only a couple of new holes in the stirrup leathers to fit Jimmy.

Slocum slid the rifle from the smaller man's saddle boot. The weapon, a Winchester 73 in .38-40 caliber, showed signs of use, but was in good condition. Slocum glanced at the initials "EC" carved into the stock of the rifle, wondered idly what name they represented, then pushed the thought aside.

The saddlebags yielded thirty rounds of ammunition for the rifle and forty for the smaller man's handgun, a Colt Lightning double-action revolver in .41 long caliber with bird's-head grips of carved ivory. The balance was awkward in Slocum's hand, but he was accustomed to a heavier, more substantial handgun. He handed the revolver to the wide-eyed youngster.

"Ever fire a handgun, Jimmy?"

"Dad let me shoot his old Remington cap-and-ball a few times," Jimmy said, flipping the loading gate open and ejecting the cartridges before examining the weapon. "Never could hit much with it."

"It takes work to be a good handgun shot. I'll work with you until you're comfortable with it."

Jimmy looked up at Slocum. "You'll teach me that fast draw?"

"No. Speed isn't the important thing, Jimmy." He didn't add that he had no intention of starting the young man down the trail of the fast-draw gun hawk. That trail got too rocky. "Putting the slug where it will do the most good is. It's the same thing as shooting a rifle in that respect. Accuracy with that first shot is the objective. You're a rifleman by nature, Jimmy, and the handgun is for close-in work. Speaking of rifles, here's your new one." He handed the .38-40 to the boy.

Jimmy stroked the smooth-worn stock of the Winchester, cleared the chamber, then swung the rifle to his shoulder. He didn't take aim at anything, just getting accustomed to the weapon. "Feels good. Stock's a bit long to fit, though."

"That's easy enough to fix. We'll take care of it later." Slocum watched the boy with care, and was pleased at how he handled weapons with studied respect; within minutes, Slocum knew he wouldn't have to worry about Jimmy carelessly shooting one or the other of them. The kid had been well-schooled in that area. Carelessness killed more people than deliberate trigger pulls.

The boy's stock grew still more in Slocum's eyes. He'd do to ride with despite his tender years. Common sense seemed to be a natural, inborn trait. Some were born with it; others never acquired it if they lived to be ninety. Jimmy had it, much to Slocum's relief.

"Any experience with rifles other than your .22?" Slocum asked.

"Some," Jimmy said, not looking up from the rifle in his hands. "Dad let me use his old .56 Spencer when we went huntin'. Shot it maybe six, seven times. It didn't shoot all that far, but a man worked in close enough to a deer and hit it in the right spot, the deer went down."

"That's the name of the game, Jimmy. Know your weapon's limitations and get close enough to place the shot. You can practice with the rifle later. Right now, I'd sort of like to get this stuff loaded and put a few miles between us and this place."

Concern flickered in Jimmy's eyes when he lifted his gaze to Slocum. "Think there might be more of them?"

"Probably not," Slocum said. "These two look like loners. But I never did care for 'probably.' That's a word that can get a man killed. Which horse do you want?"

Jimmy studied the two hobbled animals. "The sorrel."

"He looks a bit antsy," Slocum said. "Not much more than a green bronc. Could be hard to handle."

"We'll get along. The blue roan's big and stout, but the sorrel's quicker. Probably faster."

"You know your horses, partner."

"When you have—had—a cavalryman for a daddy, you learn about horses," Jimmy said. He nodded toward the two bodies. The heavy buzz of blowflies already droned in the clearing, drawn by the scent of blood and death. "We gonna bury them?"

Slocum shrugged. "Doesn't seem to me like they deserve it. Coyotes and buzzards have to eat too. And if they've got friends, it could cost us time we might not have. Of course, if it bothers you—"

Jimmy shook his head. "I reckon not. Buried my folks as best I could, which wasn't much, but I don't suppose we owe these two nothin'."

"Okay, let's strip the younger man. Maybe you can wear his clothes. You need a hat anyway. His boots might fit too. Let's get to work."

A half hour later, the two turned their backs to the camp on the creek. The sorrel fidgeted some when Jimmy swung into the dead man's saddle, but settled down under the boy's steady hand.

The bronc streak in the sorrel worried Slocum a bit at first. The dead man's boots were a bit too tight across the instep for Jimmy, and he rode now in the shoes Slocum had patched. The flat heels of farm shoes weren't meant to hold a stirrup. If anything happened and a heel slipped through a stirrup, the boy could be hung up. Being dragged and kicked to death was a hell of a messy way to go. Slocum would feel better about it after they found a good bootmaker who could stretch out the dead man's boots to fit the boy. Meantime, he'd just have to keep a close watch on the sorrel.

The blue roan trotted behind Slocum's bay on lead, bedrolls and possibles sacks strapped across the gelding's broad back.

"Slocum?"

"Yes?"

"Now that we've got camp stuff and I've got a horse, we can move fast. Maybe find those men's tracks real soon."

Slocum turned in the saddle and smiled at the boy. "They've still got too big a lead on us, Jimmy. We could spend two lifetimes riding and never cut their trail. One thing you'll have to learn in this business is patience. We'll come up with a plan when we camp for the night. There's a good spot about six hours south of here, across the Cimarron."

Slocum leaned back against his saddle as the sun dipped low in the west and listened to the first sounds of night-prowling animals and the rustle of the dying wind through the leaves of elm and cottonwood trees flanking the cool, fresh waters of the deep spring. The camp was one of Slocum's favorite spots when he happened to wander through this country. It had been used for centuries, by Indians, Comancheros, Mexican shepherds, and buffalo hunters.

Jimmy busied himself with camp chores without having been asked. Slocum was pleased that the youngster carried his share of the load—and that he hadn't wasted a lot of time playing with his new weapons. The kid wasn't gun-crazy. That was another good sign.

He'd only asked one question about the guns along the way: "Do I have to get rid of my .22?"

"No," Slocum said. "It's a good camp meat gun, and I'm hoping you'll be the hunter of this outfit most of the time. We'll rig a way for you to carry both rifles."

"Be glad to do the huntin'," Jimmy answered with a solemn nod, the brim of the slightly oversized hat snugged down around his ears against the wind. "I'm pretty good at it." It wasn't a boyish boast, just a statement of fact.

As he sipped coffee and watched Jimmy work, Slocum gave the rifle taken from the big man's saddle boot more than that first quick, cursory glance.

He had noticed the length of the weapon when the one-eyed man had first ridden up. The rifle was a Peabody .44-95, its solid heft perfectly balanced. A long-range shooter's piece, single-shot, with a ladder-type tang sight folded against the grip behind the receiver.

Slocum had fired a Peabody before. He knew what it would do. The odd-looking, tapered, and then bottlenecked cartridge could put a slug on target at a thousand yards if the man behind the trigger did his part. And the heavy 470-grain slug hit with a hell of a wallop.

Slocum had wasted little more than a glance on the big man's handgun before tossing it into a brush clump. The battered Smith & Wesson American was little more than a piece of junk, with its shot-out barrel and worn cylinder latch that could fail at any moment. It wasn't worth four bits.

The rifle, he'd keep.

The Winchester .44-40 Slocum carried was a fine, accurate rifle, and its lever-action design could send a lot of lead downrange in a hurry—but only to a couple hundred yards with any punch and accuracy. The single-shot Peabody would drop a man almost as far away as the shooter could see him. He found a full box of twenty cartridges for the long rifle in the man's saddlebags.

Slocum reluctantly sheathed the Peabody, rose, and went to help Jimmy sort out the rest of the equipment.

"Slocum," Jimmy said as they worked, "have you been thinkin' on what we're goin' to do?"

"Yes, I have. The first thing is to see if we can find out who we're after. That'll give us a starting place to figure out their habits, where they like to hole up, or where they might be headed."

The boy's sunburned brow wrinkled. "How do we do that?"

"I've got a few contacts. We'll swing south by east to Jacksboro, put the word out, rest up a couple of days. Then we'll pick up a few more things we need before we head out."

"You have friends there, Slocum? In this Jacksboro place?"

Slocum half smiled. "Yes." He didn't add that there was one friend in particular he intended to call on. Jimmy savvied a lot for a kid, but some things were best not talked on.

3

Jacksboro had changed some in the last three years, Slocum mused as he and Jimmy rode into town on the Doan's Crossing trail from the northwest.

The town had grown, or at least spread out; the tents and rickety clapboard shacks had given way to sturdy, more permanent structures made of native stone or smoothly hewn timber. The streets were still crowded, but without the crush of people—of all stripes—who had jammed into the town during the days when Jacksboro had marked the westering edge of Comanche country.

A smattering of blue-uniformed soldiers mingled with the civilians along the streets, but not nearly as many as when Fort Richardson, a mile to the south, had been the staging area for Ranald Mackenzie's 4th Cavalry preparing for the long campaign to sweep the Comanches from the Staked Plains.

Mackenzie's fighting troops, infantry and cavalry alike, now were mostly far to the northwest, intent on putting down a possible Ute uprising; the soldiers left behind held garrison duty, a force in name only, more to reassure the merchants and townsmen of Jacksboro that the army hadn't abandoned them to the raids from reservation-jumping warriors in Indian Territory a few hours' ride to the north.

Slocum glanced at the boy riding alongside. Jimmy's eyes were wide, his gaze darting from one place to another. Slocum saw the faint touch of apprehension in the set of the boy's jaw.

Finally, Jimmy turned to Slocum.

"I never seen so many people in one place," Jimmy said. "Matter of fact, I never been to a real town before. Not a big town anyway. Slocum, what do all these people do?"

"Lots of things, Jimmy. Buy, sell, and trade stuff mostly. Just make a living as best they can, like people anywhere."

"But there's so many of 'em." The boy's knuckles whitened as his fingers tensed on the bridle reins. "Makes me feel—I don't know—crowded, I guess. Like I don't have no room to breathe."

Slocum nodded, barely suppressing a smile. "I feel the same way in towns, Jimmy. Big ones or small ones. But a man can get things he needs in town that he can't on the trail most times." He didn't tell Jimmy that towns were more dangerous than the open frontier. The boy had enough on his mind at it was.

"What'll we do now, Slocum?"

"Stable the horses, find a hotel room, stow our gear, then hunt up a barbershop with a bathtub. Both of us need to shed some trail grit. Then we'll go call on an acquaintance of mine. If anybody can help us find out who raided your place, he can."

Jimmy scrubbed a finger behind his earlobe. "Reckon I could stand a bath at that."

And before too many more months had passed, an occasional shave, Slocum thought. James Daniel Forrest was growing up in a hurry. In the short time they had ridden together, Slocum had fallen into the easy habit of talking with Jimmy as a grown man. He'd had to remind himself at times that Jimmy was still just a youngster.

Jimmy hadn't objected when Slocum asked him to stow the .41 Lightning in the saddlebags before riding into town. He did it first, then asked why—not in a complaining way, but from simple curiosity.

"Because," Slocum said, "a man should never carry a handgun openly unless he intends to use it, and he should never shoot unless he intends to kill. Besides, wearing a gun just invites trouble.''

"You wear yours all the time."

Slocum nodded. "I wish I didn't have to, Jimmy," he said softly. He let it drop at that.

Dub Packer leaned back in the creaky chair of the cramped sheriff's office, bushy gray brows bunched as he listened to Jimmy's story.

Slocum knew Packer was pushing sixty, and for four decades of those years he had worn a star. The fact that he'd lived so long in a dangerous trade was enough to establish the man as rawhide tough. When Dub Packer had an arrest warrant, as often as not he simply sent word to the wanted man to come in. If the fugitive knew Packer, he usually came in. Nobody wanted Packer, who actually was the grandfather that he looked to be, coming after them in person. Best of all, Packer had developed the best network of information sources west of the Mississippi. Sources on both sides of the law and both sides of the border.

"So," Packer said in his low, rumbling baritone as Jimmy finished his story, "you're after a half dozen men you've never seen?"

"Yes, sir. Well, I never seen 'em personal, but I know a few things about 'em," Jimmy said.

"I'm listening." Packer steepled his fingers and leaned forward, elbows on the scarred, paper-cluttered desk.

At Jimmy's glance, Slocum nodded. "Go ahead. Tell it just as you told me."

The boy turned his attention back to the lawman. "One of 'em rides a white horse, I think maybe an albino. I found some tail hairs hung up in a bush where they'd camped."

Packer nodded. "Could help. Not that many pure white horses around, and even fewer albinos. Go ahead, son."

Jimmy's brow furrowed in thought. "Another man rides a big, stout red roan, a good sixteen hands high. Probably a full-blood Morgan, judging from the size of the foot. The Morgan's got a funny set to the off front foot—toes out something fierce, like maybe he'd had a hurt fetlock sometime." The boy paused for a moment, then continued. "Man who rides that horse, a big one if the rest of him fits his boot tracks, is crippled. Right foot's bent way over to the side. Walks almost up on his ankle. That help any?"

Packer glanced at Slocum, surprise apparent in the pale blue eyes, then turned his gaze back to the boy. "It helps. You pick up on all this from a few days' tracking, son?"

"Yes, sir. I hunt a lot. Man can't hunt if he can't track."

"You're right there. Anything else?"

"Yes, sir. There's a one-armed man ridin' with 'em. I found an old wore-out shirt he'd throwed away. Used to be blue. Had a dark stain low on the left side, like dried blood. One sleeve—the left—was cut off and sewed shut just above the elbow. Found this too, at the house."

Jimmy fished in his pocket, brought out a stubby metallic case, and handed it to the sheriff. "There was other empties layin' around, but this one was different."

Packer examined the spent cartridge case for a moment, then glanced up at Slocum. "Forty-six Short rimfire. Mighty scarce round these days. Haven't seen one for years. Anything else come to mind?"

Jimmy thought for a moment, then shook his head. "Reckon that's it. Might be somethin' I ain't rememberin' right now."

"Okay. I'll put the word out, along with a description of your sister and the stolen stock. It may take a couple of days, maybe more. If I can get a line on them at all."

Packer nodded toward Slocum. "You ought to pick your travelin' partners better, Jimmy." A quick, slight grin twitched the edges of Packer's full handlebar mustache. "This worthless saddle tramp is nothing but trouble waiting to happen."

Slocum winked at Jimmy. "You just heard the kettle call the pot black, Jimmy. This man wasn't always as mellowed out and mild-mannered as he is now. Of course, that was before he got old and soft in the belly. Much obliged for helping out, Dub."

Packer rose and offered his hand to the boy first, then Slocum. "No need to thank me just yet. Haven't done anything. Check back with me from time to time. I don't get out of the office much anymore, so I'll likely be here. Do me a favor, Slocum? Stay out of trouble. I'd hate like the dickens to have to run you out of town again.''

Slocum touched his hat brim. "I'll do my best, Sheriff. By the way, Jesus Quintana still in town? Looked like his shop was empty when we rode by.''

"He's still here, and still the best bootmaker this side of El Paso. Just moved. Across from the Trailhead Saloon, west two doors down.''

As the man and boy stepped into the late afternoon sunlight and stood waiting for a break in the traffic to cross the street, Dub Packer stood at the window, watching.

If that boy ever decides to go into law work, Packer thought, I'll pin a badge on him myself. Most deputies couldn't read track on a five-legged buffalo. The kid had picked up as much information from the tracks as most grown men would have if they'd seen the raiders close up in person. White or albino horse, a one-armed man—who'd maybe been shot recently—another mount with a splayed-out off front hoof ridden by a cripple, and somebody who packed a rimfire Forty-six Short side arm. And traveling with a girl, if they hadn't killed her already. Shouldn't be too hard to get a line on that bunch. He turned away from the window and started thumbing through a stack of flyers on the cluttered desk.

As they threaded their way across the busy street, Jimmy cast a worried glance at Slocum. "The sheriff didn't write none of that down, what I told him.''

"He doesn't need to, Jimmy. I don't know how he does it, but Dub Packer can still remember every man he ever met and most of every conversation he's ever had.''

Jimmy stepped onto the crude boardwalk on the south side of the street. "Is that right, what the sheriff said? Did he really run you out of town?''

"Well, he asked me politely if I wouldn't mind sort of easing out of Junction City up in Colorado a few years back.''

"And you went? Just like that?''

"Just like that,'' Slocum said. "Dub Packer never backs a man into a corner, but when he asks him to do something, it's in the man's best interest to do it.''

Jimmy sniffed. "How come? He's old, and he can't be as good with a gun as you are, Slocum."

Slocum put a hand on the youth's shoulder. "Don't judge a man by his age or looks. And as to who's the best with a gun, me or Dub Packer, I don't intend to find out, Jimmy. Neither does Dub." He dropped his hand and led the way toward the hotel. "We'll leave your boots with Quintana to be stretched."

Slocum caught the almost imperceptible hesitation in Jimmy's stride, the quick sideways glance, as they strode past a store window with its display of stick candy. It reminded Slocum again that Jimmy was still a kid.

"Go ahead, Jimmy," Slocum said. "A man's got to give in to his wants from time to time, or he's apt to pop right open."

"But it costs money, Slocum. I—we—may need every penny before this is over with."

"I don't think a nickel's going to make that much difference, partner. Use the money we took from those two owl-hoots. Go ahead. Enjoy yourself."

Slocum waited until Jimmy emerged from the store, a stick of hard, striped candy already tucked into the corner of his mouth and four more in his shirt pocket. He offered one to Slocum.

"No, thanks, Jimmy. By the way, you may be on your own for most of the night. I have some wants of my own to tend."

Wariness flickered in the boy's gaze. "Slocum, you ain't going to get drunk on me, are you? I ain't got the money to go bail if you get throwed in jail."

Slocum smiled. "No. Did that once. Didn't like the way it felt the next day. I may have a couple of drinks—on my own money, of course—but I promise I'll behave myself."

At the boy's nod, Slocum said, "There are some good cafes near the hotel. You can get a good supper for less than a quarter. Don't scrimp on the meal to save money. We'll get by. You have your own key to the hotel room. I may be late getting in, so don't wait up. And don't shoot me when I do come back."

* * *

Slocum hesitated for a moment before the small one-story building just off Jacksboro's main east-west street. At one time it had been one of the finer homes in Jacksboro, not wide but deep, built of native rock that kept the interior cool in summer and warm in winter.

The neat, precise block lettering on the window still read, "Hanna's," and in smaller script, "Tailoring and Alterations." That didn't mean Hanna Einreich still owned the place. Or that she was still unmarried.

There was one way to find out.

Slocum pushed the door open, heard the tinkle of a small bell as the door frame jostled the metal, and stepped inside. He saw no one, but a few seconds later heard the familiar voice from a curtained side room:

"Be with you in just a moment!"

Slocum's heartbeat quickened. Hanna was still here, at least. He waited, becoming somewhat uncomfortable as he stood amid the feminine-shaped wire and wood fitting forms, two of them clad in petticoats and stayed corsets. He'd never been shy around women, but all the undergarments on display left him feeling as out of place as a jackass in a chicken coop.

The soft murmur of voices came from behind the curtain. "That should do it, Mrs. Galliman." Hanna's words became more audible as the curtain swung open. "Your gown will be ready in two days."

Two women stepped from behind the curtain. The younger, shorter one glanced at Slocum; her brows went up and her blue eyes widened. "I'll be right with you, sir," she said. "Thank you for your patience." The words were calm and professional, but seemed a bit breathless.

The older woman silently sniffed at Slocum, apparently offended that a lowly male should invade the sanctity of an expensive ladies' stitchery, then promptly ignored his presence. "Hanna, I simply *must* have that gown by the weekend officers' ball. You know how important that is. Why, it's the social event of the season, and everyone in town who is anyone will be there. Are you quite positive it will be ready?"

Hanna reached up and put a hand on the woman's shoulder. "It will be, Mrs. Galliman, and you will be the most glamorous woman at the ball. Why, your dance card will be filled with the names of dashing young officers just minutes after you arrive.''

Hanna gently steered the gray-haired woman to the door, and waved a cheery good-bye as Mrs. Galliman strode toward a shiny new black buggy where a uniformed Negro driver waited patiently.

Hanna closed the door, leaned her shoulders against it, hands behind the small of her back, and grinned at Slocum.

"Slocum, you long-legged bastard, I saw you ride past earlier. My heart jumped clear up in my throat. Then I started getting a little put out with you. I'd about decided you weren't going to come see me.''

"You should know better than that, Hanna. I just had a few chores to tend first.'' His gaze swept her from head to toe. "You haven't changed a bit.'' Which was, Slocum had to admit, close enough to the truth. The top of Hanna's head barely reached Slocum's shoulder, and she still carried the stamp of her German peasant heritage, the stocky, muscular body, the round face that now showed only the faintest wrinkles.

"You are smooth-talking, lying son of a bitch, Slocum,'' she said, her voice soft and husky. "What's it been? Three, four years?''

"Thereabouts, give or take six months either way. Seems a lot longer.'' Slocum became aware of the tension beginning to stir in his groin. The woman with the short-cropped golden hair and teasingly mischievous cornflower-blue eyes always had that effect on him.

"Yes, it does,'' she said. "Seem a lot longer. A hell of a lot longer.'' Somewhere in the back of the shop, a mantel clock bonged six times. "Excuse me a minute.'' She turned, barred the door, and picked up a block-lettered sign that read, "Closed, please call again.'' She propped the sign in the window and carefully drew the drapes.

Seconds later she barreled into Slocum. Her arms went around his waist. She buried her face in his chest. The embrace lingered as if both of them were content for the moment to simply soak up the feel, the warmth, of each other. Slocum savored her scent of lilac water and the faint, underlying tinge of woman musk.

After a time, Hanna drew her head and shoulders back, lifted herself onto her tiptoes, and stared deep into Slocum's eyes. The teasing twinkle had faded from her gaze, a sultry look of want pushing it aside. Slocum lowered his head and kissed her, gently at first, then longer, more urgently. Her lips, soft and moist, parted, and the tip of her tongue slipped between his teeth. Her breathing and Slocum's quickened; Slocum felt the press of her ample breasts through the thin cloth of his shirt.

Finally, Hanna broke the kiss, her nostrils flared, her breath coming in shallow, quick gasps as she lowered her head back onto his chest. Slocum felt the rapid thump of her heart against the palm of his hand, which rested high on her rib cage.

She muttered something in the deep, guttural German tongue that always mystified Slocum; he spoke fluent Spanish, and passable Comanche, Cheyenne, and half a dozen other Indian languages, but German was beyond his grasp.

After she finally stopped, Slocum put a finger beneath her jaw and lifted her face. "I don't know what you just said, so I don't know whether to be offended or not," he said.

Mischief twinkled again in the blue eyes. "I refuse to translate, but I promise you it wasn't an insult." She stepped back and took his hand. "I assume you still enjoy a touch of the distilled spirits, the work of the devil, from time to time?"

"On special occasions. Like now."

Her laugh was soft, musical despite its huskiness. "Me too. I shall, sir, offer you a drink at this time."

"Ma'am, I'd be delighted to accept." Slocum tried to ignore the swelling in his Levi's, but without much success.

She looped her arm beneath his, the pressure and warmth of her breast against his biceps, and led him past the stacks of cloth and other accoutrements of her trade to a door at the back of the shop. She toed it open. Her dress and petticoats rustled at the brief motion.

Slocum noticed she hadn't changed her living quarters in back of the shop. That was like Hanna, he mused; once she found the right place for something, she didn't go moving it about randomly the way some women did.

The back of the shop consisted of a combination kitchen and dining area with a couple of overstuffed chairs on the far wall facing a small wood-burning stove and, behind a door that stood open, the oversized, neatly made bed that dominated the smaller bedroom. The place was spotlessly clean, a trait Slocum had observed among the few others of German descent he had known.

Hanna released Slocum's arm, lifted onto her tiptoes, opened a cabinet door, and pulled out a quart bottle of Old Overholt. She cocked an eyebrow at Slocum. "Your favorite brand, I seem to recall from long ago and faraway days."

"You recall well, Hanna."

She chuckled. "It wasn't hard to remember that. This is the same bottle you left here last time. It should be well aged by now." She nodded toward a sturdy mahogany china cabinet. "Fetch a couple of glasses and bring an ashtray. I've got to get out of these damn petticoats. Make me sweat like a pig." She led the way into the bedroom.

"Pour a couple," Hanna said, nodding toward a small round table beside the bed. "I'm going to wash up a bit—added a bathing room since you were here last. Make yourself at home. I'll be back in a minute."

Slocum poured a double shot into each of the glasses, then perched on the edge of the soft, feathery bed, sipped at the whiskey, and tried to ignore the whisper of cloth and soft splash of water from beyond the door to the bathing room where Hanna had disappeared. The scent of lilac lingered in the air of the bedroom. The lowering sun sent a soft, gentle, filtered light through the lone window above the headboard.

After a few minutes the door swung open. Slocum stopped in the act of lifting his drink, the glass held just below his chin.

Hanna leaned against the door frame, hip cocked, clad in a thin, pale blue housedress that clung to her sturdy body. The nipples of her heavy breasts pushed against the cloth; despite the fullness, the small points were in the right place, just at the forward tip, with no hint of sagging. A deep shadow fell between the mounds of flesh where the top two buttons of her dress remained open.

Slocum let his gaze move over her slowly, savoring the sight. For a short woman, she carried an unexpected amount of flesh—but all of it was muscular and firm. Beneath the slightly thick waist, broad hips flared above muscular legs that tapered to trim, almost delicate, ankles and small feet.

"Well, you lecherous saddle tramp, did you pour me a drink, or were you going to finish the bottle yourself?" She strode to Slocum, hips swaying with each stride, perched on the bed beside him, and took the glass he held out. Slocum never ceased to wonder how those short, almost stubby fingers could work such delicate magic with a needle.

Hanna downed a hefty swallow of whiskey, took his glass, and placed both drinks on the bedside table. She twisted her torso and nuzzled Slocum's neck. He felt the quickening of her breath against his skin, the soft firmness of her breasts. The swelling in Slocum's crotch grew. After a minute or two, she lifted her head and kissed him, deep and fiery.

Slocum's hand drifted from her cheek down her shoulder, and brushed the swell of her warm breast; his palm gently stroked the swollen nipple through the thin cloth. Her breath caught in her throat; she seemed to shiver slightly.

Then she broke the kiss, her blue eyes smoky above her small, upturned nose and almost square jawline. "I won't even attempt small talk now, Slocum," she said breathlessly. "I wouldn't make sense anyway. God, it's been *such* a long time—"

Hanna stood and turned to face Slocum. Her fingers went to the buttons of her dress. "Get your clothes off, Slocum, before I rip them off you. I promised myself I'd be the demure, shy type, but goddamn it, I can't help myself with you—and you aren't worth a damn to me fully dressed."

Her full breasts heaved with her heavy breathing as the last button parted and the dress fell away. Slocum sat and watched, savoring the moment despite the almost painful fullness in his crotch. It was worth the slight delay.

Hanna's nipples weren't brown, more of a deep pink tinged with dark tan, the buds erect in the center of a tannish, quarter-sized circle of pigment; her solidly fleshed thighs and slightly rounded belly met in a triangle of golden hair a bit darker and coarser than that on her head.

"My God, woman," Slocum said softly, "you're still the most gorgeous creature I've ever seen."

"Lying bastard." Her words were almost a whisper. "But I sure as hell don't mind you saying so."

Slocum shook his head in mock dismay. "Such coarse language from such a fine lady. I swear, I don't know what the world's coming to these days." He reached out, pulled her close, and stroked the firm curve of her buttocks and upper thighs.

She slapped his hand lightly. "Let go of me and strip, dammit!"

By the time Slocum had undressed, leaving the holstered Peacemaker within easy reach on the floor by the bed, Hanna had stripped the bedcover down to expose the sheets and stretched out on her side.

Slocum eased himself onto the bed and lay facing her; she immediately moved to him, the full length of her body pressed against his. She kissed him again, her tongue and soft, moist lips showing her need. Slocum stroked her breast, gently rolled the erect nipple between his fingers, and heard her half whimper of pleasure.

Her hand slipped between them, toying for a moment with his tightened scrotum; then her fingers closed around his shaft as she broke the lingering kiss. Slocum's hand drifted down her ribs to her hip, her upper thigh, and she spread her legs. She gasped aloud as his fingers drifted slowly and gently up her inner thigh to the blond triangle of hair between her legs.

He left his palm resting there a moment, feeling the damp heat against his hand. Then he softly slipped his finger between the folds of her outer lips, his fingertip resting on the small, swollen bud of her clitoris. Her hips began moving reflexively against his hand. A moan escaped from her lips and her head tilted away, back arched against his touch. Slocum massaged the bud, first up and down, then in a circular motion. Hanna's body tensed; she shuddered as her muscles convulsed. Slocum could feel the pulsing contractions as she climaxed; a pleasantly smooth slickness spread against his fingers and hand.

Slocum moved his finger from her clitoris, parted her inner lips, and slid his index finger slowly into her vagina. He had forgotten the snug fit around his one finger, and marveled at the tightness of her.

"Damn—you—quit—toying—take me, Slocum." Hanna's breath came in quick, sharp gasps. "Take me—now." She rolled onto her back, pulling Slocum atop her.

Despite her wetness and the seepage from the head of Slocum's shaft, entering her was a bit of an effort. First the head, then slowly, inch by inch, his full length until he was deeply into her. The hot, tight dampness, the pulsing of her vaginal muscles against his shaft, almost made Slocum lose it too soon. He held back, keeping himself deep inside her, for several heartbeats until he regained a measure of control, then began to move. Slowly at first, almost withdrawing, then the long, deep thrust. Her grip around his neck tightened, and her legs came up to wrap around his upper thighs. Sweat slicked their skin where breast and belly met.

Hanna's hips moved against Slocum, in time with his thrusts, becoming more urgent until their crotches met with a faint but audible sound. Then her arms and legs clamped harder around him; a series of short, whimpering half sobs, half groans sounded in his ear as her entire body convulsed. Her inner contractions massaged Slocum's shaft in quick, hard spasms.

The rapid clenching and releasing of her vaginal muscles brought Slocum to the raw edge, but still he managed to hold back. He thrust deep into Hanna, held himself there unmoving, until her breathing slowed, then began to pick up again. He managed to free his head, and by bending his neck at a sharp angle, to roll his tongue around her still-engorged left nipple.

Within moments, Hanna's body convulsed again. The soft, low moan from her throat broke into a series of short, staccato gasps; her vaginal muscles pulsed even more powerfully than before. At the peak of her orgasm, Slocum quit fighting it and exploded inside her, the deep, heavy pulses of his powerful ejaculation so intense as to border on painful, taking his breath away. His muscle-clenching spasms seemed to continue for a long time before they began to slow.

Slocum became aware that Hanna's contractions had also eased, but they still stroked his shaft as if milking the last drop from him, her legs pulling hard against his thighs to draw him as deeply into her as possible as her shudders ebbed. Finally, Slocum felt himself begin to wilt inside her. Hanna had her head back, her mouth open, gasping for breath, her arms no longer around his neck, both hands curled into fists and gripping a wad of sheet. Slowly, she began to relax.

Every joint in Slocum's body seemed to have become disconnected, his muscles weak and quavering, but he managed to keep his weight on his elbows to keep from crushing her.

He again lowered his head to tongue her left nipple, and found the pinkish-brown bud still erect. Her left hand came up and lifted his face.

"No more—Slocum," she said, a slight, relaxed grin lifting the corners of her mouth and dimpling her cheeks. "I surrender. For now."

Slocum kissed her lightly. "Just in time too. I believe you're safe from further assault, Hanna. At least for the time being." As he spoke, he felt his wet, limp shaft slip from inside her.

She kissed him back, gently, her lips speaking silently of tenderness and, Slocum thought, gratitude. Then she pushed against his shoulders. "Get your sweaty body off me, you oaf. I'm done with you anyway."

Slocum rolled off her, leaving a wet trace of fluid on her upper thigh, and lay on his back beside her, more relaxed than he had been in months. He sighed in contentment.

Hanna propped herself on an elbow, her free hand tracing the curve of Slocum's jaw. "Damn, fellow," she said, "I'd forgotten how good you are in the sack."

"You're not half bad yourself, girl," Slocum said. "Best I've ever had, in fact. Except you've got this silly grin on your face now."

"You put it there. And you're wearing one just like it. Shame on you, seducing an innocent woman in such a"—the mantel clock in the kitchen bonged seven times—"short time."

"Excuse me, ma'am, but who seduced who?"

She laughed softly. "Who the hell cares?"

"So, what now?" he asked after a moment's comfortable silence. "Small-talk time?"

She tweaked the hair on his chest. "Nope. Supper time. The least you can do is feed a lady once you're done using her."

"Could be a question of who used who, but we won't argue the point. Pick your restaurant. Of course, we'll have to get dressed first. If we're able. I'm not so sure I am."

Hanna swung her legs over the edge of the bed, sat up, and glanced down at her crotch. "What a mess. You pack a bigger load than a Mexican stud, Slocum. I think I'm drowned from the waist down."

She reached for the bottle, refilled both glasses, and handed one to him. "Here's to you, Slocum."

"And to you, Miss Hanna Einreich. I assume it's still 'Miss'? Or have you found a man?"

Hanna winked at him over the rim of her glass. "Would it make a difference to you?"

"Not unless he happened to walk in the door with a shotgun in his hand."

She downed a swallow and shook her head. "Wouldn't make any difference to me either. I must admit I tried a couple on for size. They didn't fit. You do. Now, finish that drink and feed me, you cad. I'm starved. During dinner you can tell me what you're doing here—and how long you plan to stay."

The smile faded from Slocum's lips. He downed his drink, stood on shaky legs, and reached for his clothing. "I can't answer the last part of your question just yet, Hanna. A lot depends on what Dub Packer finds out."

4

Slocum leaned back against the pillow and stared into the half-closed blue eyes inches from his own.

In the early afternoon light from the window above the bed, the skin of Hanna's round face held the pinkish tinge of exertion and the contentment of release. Sweat plastered stray strands of her harvest-gold hair into ringlets against her neck and set the window light glistening across her ample breasts. A gentle smile lifted the corners of her lips, dimpling her full cheeks.

"Did I happen to mention you are a very attractive young lady?" Slocum asked.

"Save the sweet talk, you long-legged bastard," Hanna scolded, but the glint in her eyes acknowledged the compliment. "You're not getting any more. I'm not only caught up, I'm wiped out—and getting a little bit sore. So I'm done with you. Go talk your way between some other innocent girl's legs."

Slocum grinned and winked. "Couldn't help her a bit, Hanna. Not even you. Innocence and all. Not now."

"You lie like a sleeping hound, Slocum. You recover quicker than a buck rabbit. If I were of a mind to, I'd bet a double eagle I could have you back in action in ten minutes. But I've got to wash up and go to work. Girl's got to make a dollar now and then."

Slocum felt a moment of remorse. "Sorry. I've kept you from your work, and you've got to finish Mrs. What's-her-name's gown—" Her finger over his lips shushed him.

"It was my idea, Slocum. And a damn find one it was. Besides, it won't take a half hour to finish Mrs. Galliman's dress. I let the rich biddies think a lot more work is involved than there really is. That way, they'll think they're getting their money's worth when I overcharge the hell out of them."

Slocum grinned. "I'm not surprised. Nobody ever said you didn't have a mind for business."

"When I have my mind on business, I get by." She muttered something in guttural German. Slocum thought the words sounded a bit like the southern Comanche dialect.

"Should I ask what you just said?"

"Just something about handsome studs and perfectly mar-velous afternoons," Hanna said languidly, nuzzling his neck. She lifted a hand and pushed a finger against her left nipple. "Down, damn you," she scolded the erect button. "You've had enough."

Slocum chuckled as Hanna eased herself from the bed and reached for the damp cloth and towel on the bedside table. She cleaned herself, tossed the cold damp rag onto Slocum's belly, and grinned as he loosed a startled squawk.

"Wouldn't hurt you to go to work either." Her grin faded. "It's time you checked in on Jimmy. The poor child. What he's been through . . ." Her voice trailed away for a moment. "I hope you find those men, Slocum. And the girl. Alive and well."

"With a little luck, we'll find them. I can't be too optimistic about getting Jimmy's sister back. Or what shape she might be in if we do," Slocum said. "Maybe Dub's turned up some-thing by now."

"If he has, you'll be leaving." It wasn't a question. It was a statement. Her words held a Germanic stoicism and a tinge of regret. At Slocum's silent nod, she said, "Will you come back when it's—over?"

"If I can," Slocum said with a gentle smile. "There's no place I'd rather be than right here."

"I'll be waiting."

Slocum dried himself, dressed, kissed her lightly on the lips, and let himself out the back door.

Jimmy was waiting patiently, sitting on the back stoop and tracing lines in the alley dirt with the blade tip of his pocket knife. Slocum wondered what the boy had heard. Hanna was no screamer, but she still wasn't exactly silent when she was having a good time.

"Sheriff wants us," Jimmy said without expression. He wiped the blade against his pants, folded it, and slipped the knife into his pocket. "Says he's got some information."

"How long have you been waiting, Jimmy?" Slocum asked as the two strode toward Packer's office a few blocks away.

The youth shrugged. "Not long."

"How did you know where to find me?"

Jimmy shrugged again. "Wasn't that hard." Slocum couldn't tell from the boy's tone if he was angry with him, disappointed, or maybe a bit jealous; Slocum conceded he hadn't spent as much time with Jimmy as he should have since they'd ridden into Jacksboro.

Dub Packer sat behind his desk, a scowl on his weathered face. Slocum thought the sheriff looked mad at the whole world. "Took you long enough, son," he said, a bit grumpily.

"Slocum was busy. We're here now."

Packer's stern features softened a bit. "Sorry, Jimmy. I didn't mean to snap at you." He shifted his gaze to Slocum. "I've got a line on your man, Slocum. Don't see how it could be anybody else but Dirk Dunnigan."

The name cut into Slocum's gut like a Bowie knife. His jaw muscles clenched and his eyes narrowed. "Shiloh Dunnigan?"

"One and the same." The bitterness in the sheriff's voice matched Slocum's. "Slocum, my legal jurisdiction ends at the county line. But where that son of a bitch is concerned, my jurisdiction runs from here to the gates of Hell. Say the word and I'll go with you. Or I can have four or forty good men, all veterans, in the saddle in two hours."

Slocum ignored the cold knot of hate and rage in his gut. He shook his head. "A posse's out of the question. He'd spot that many men from twenty miles off. And kill the girl. Two men can do the job better and quieter—Jimmy and me. We're going to get her back alive.'' If she still is, he thought. He didn't say so out loud.

Packer nodded in understanding. He'd tracked down enough men, red and white, to know when one hunter was enough and two cavalry companies weren't. "I'll be honest with you, Slocum. I want that bastard dead—and dead the hard way— as bad as you do, just like anybody else who ever wore a uniform. On either side. I'd like to go with you.''

"No, Dub. There isn't a man I'd rather have, and you know it. But you've got a lot of people here who need you. And this is our fight.'' Slocum glanced at Jimmy. Questions danced in the boy's eyes, but he held his tongue in check. "What did you find out about the men with him and where they might be headed?''

Packer's chair creaked as he leaned back. "After Nebraska, they went south by southwest, crossed the Cimarron and Canadian Rivers, then headed due west. Hit a Mexican trading post at Cuero, New Mexico. Killed four people there, sacked the store, and rode on to the Pecos Valley.'' The sheriff paused to light the pipe he had been filling as he spoke. "Raided a few isolated farms and ranches there. When the locals took offense and started hunting him, Dunnigan headed west again through the San Andreas range, then cut south toward Mexico.''

When Packer paused again, puffing at his pipe, Jimmy said, "Sheriff, can I ask a question? How do you know all this?''

"The best friend a lawman ever had, son. The telegraph. I've got a stack of messages here that tracks most every place they hit along the way.'' Packer's gaze shifted to Slocum. "Slocum, when you get that son of a bitch, bring his head back here and I'll personally see you get the reward money. Five hundred dollars. Now, about the men with him . . .''

A half hour later, Slocum and Jimmy stepped from the sheriff's office into the sultry heat and swirling dust of the busy street.

"Are we going after them now?'' Jimmy asked.

"As soon as we get our gear together and pick up the supplies we'll need.''

"Slocum, I don't have much money left—"

"Don't worry about it, Jimmy. This is as much my fight now as it is yours." Slocum stopped beside the barred window of a gunsmith's shop. "See to the horses. And don't forget to pick up your boots at Quintana's. I'll get the stuff we need and meet you at the hotel in about an hour."

Jimmy nodded, then hesitated for a moment. "Slocum, you're not telling me something about this Dunnigan. How come you hate him so much?"

"It's a long story, Jimmy. There'll be plenty of time to tell it when we're on his trail. It's going to be a long, hard ride."

Still, the boy stalled, his patched shoes scuffing the dust. Without looking up, he said, "Slocum, a few more minutes won't make a difference. Say good-bye to her if you want. She's real pretty." Then Jimmy turned and strode toward the bootmaker's shop. It seemed to Slocum there was a fresh spring, an eagerness, in the boy's step.

Slocum knew how Jimmy felt. It was time to be doing something. Anything. The walls of Jacksboro's buildings seemed to close even tighter around him; towns were no place for a man of the plains and mountains. He ignored the curious stare of a young infantry private lounging nearby. Slocum was accustomed to attracting attention. A man who stood six feet two, with jet-black hair, green eyes, the lean build of a mountain cat, and who wore his handgun cross-draw style, always seemed to draw attention.

Slocum was used to it. He ignored it. That didn't mean he had to like it.

He pushed open the door of the gunsmith's shop.

Two days and almost a hundred miles southwest of Jacksboro, Slocum squatted beside a pool of fresh water at the edge of a small stream that twisted along a sandy creek flanked by stands of elm trees, cottonwoods, and junipers and a lone pecan tree.

They had left the post-oak belt behind a few hours ago. The thick stands of stubby trees and rocky, broken hills had given way to more open, rolling prairie, dotted with scattered mottes of timber. In the next few days' ride, trees and drinkable water would become progressively more scarce.

Slocum glanced at the sky, and sniffed the southwest breeze with its thin haze of dust. There was no sign of rain either in the wind or in the lowering sun in the still-brassy sky. Already the prairie grass had browned beneath the wind and grinding sun. If it didn't rain soon, Slocum knew, the country into which they rode could be a more relentless and dangerous foe than a full regiment of Dirk Dunnigans. He pushed the thoughts aside. No use expecting either the best or the worst, just things as they were.

Jimmy waited patiently a few yards downstream, where he had led the horses to drink. The boy still was something of a puzzle to Slocum. At times, it was as if Jimmy were a man grown, trail-smart and mature beyond his years. Other times, when Slocum awakened to hear him sobbing in the night, or when Jimmy thought Slocum wasn't looking and tears of loss and hurt welled in his eyes, or when he exuberantly booted his horse into a short run after a rabbit just for the sheer fun of it, Jimmy was a kid to the core.

Most of his waking hours, he was a man—solemn, soft-spoken, quiet of foot on the stalk, his spurs already earned as a hunter and tracker. And a quick student of the gun.

Jimmy would never be a true *pistolero,* but with a bit more practice he could be as good as most men.

It was with the long gun that Jimmy shone, whether the rifle he shouldered was the little .22 Remington or the .38-40 Winchester. He could place his shots where he wanted, and now he understood the effective range of the Winchester and what the weapon could and could not do.

While putting Jimmy through his paces, Slocum had fired half a dozen rounds through the Peabody .44-95, and was impressed. The rifle was accurate to better than a thousand yards, five times that of the maximum effective reach of Slocum's .44-40 lever gun. That could come in handy when they caught up with Dunnigan.

Slocum felt a tinge of sadness for the boy. Jimmy had been forced to grow up a hell of a lot faster than he should have. A kid should have time to be a kid, not be forced into a man's role before he is scarcely big enough to saddle and mount his own horse. Slocum had known such young men before. Most turned out all right. A few became walking powder kegs, ready to explode, and you couldn't tell by looking if the fuse was lit.

Slocum suspected Jimmy was one of the strong ones. The survivors accepted the cards as they fell and made the most of it, instead of blowing up because life had dealt them a hand from the bottom of the deck.

Slocum shook himself from his reverie and set about building a fire. As he pulled supplies from the packs and started their evening meal, Jimmy tethered the horses in a patch of parched but thick grass alongside the stream, then rubbed down and curried each animal in turn. It wasn't something Slocum had to tell him to do; it seemed to be a natural instinct.

The sun slid beneath the horizon as they ate, leaving behind a wash of crimson and gold across the western sky. The meal passed in silence, another thing that made Jimmy a good trail partner. He didn't jabber constantly, and when he did speak it was because he had something to say. Few things irritated Slocum more than a man in love with his own voice.

After all utensils except the coffeepot and their two tin campaign cups were washed and stowed, Slocum lit a cigarillo as Jimmy sucked on a stick of peppermint candy in the faint light of the low fire.

"Jimmy," Slocum finally said, "I'm going to have to go back on part of our deal."

The boy's back stiffened. "You're not going to quit on me, are you?"

"No, not that. Not that at all." Slocum dragged at the thin Mexican cigar and let the smoke trickle from his nostrils. "I promised you that after we get your sister back, the men who took her were yours for the killing. We're still going to get her back. But after that comes the time I have to break part of my promise. I'm going to kill Dirk Dunnigan myself."

The youth nodded. "I sort of figured as much, from the way you and the sheriff talked back in town. You said you'd tell me about this Dunnigan somewhere along the trail."

"Now's as good a time as any, Jimmy." Slocum paused to refill his coffee cup. "It dates back to the war. Have you ever heard of the 'Butcher of Shiloh'?"

Jimmy thought for a moment, then shook his head. "Dad never talked about the war."

"That man was Dirk Dunnigan. He was a corporal in the Confederate army. When the first shots were fired at Shiloh, he turned and ran. Never fired a shot at an armed enemy. But he didn't stay gone." A quiet, cold hate tinged Slocum's tone. "When night fell, he and a couple of his friends slipped back onto the battlefield. They stole money from the dead of both sides, even pulled the gold teeth from the mouths of brave men who died there. But that wasn't the worst."

Slocum paused to sip his coffee. The hot liquid seemed to add fuel to the warmth of disgust and rekindled rage in his gut. "Somehow, in the confusion of the battle, no one saw him break and run away. Or if someone did, they either died in the fight or were too tired to mention it. And his company commander was dead on the field.

"A lot of Union prisoners were taken in the Shiloh fight," Slocum said. "Dunnigan and his troop were assigned to guard nearly a hundred of them. He took it on his own to march them well away from camp, a dozen at a time, with several of his friends along. He had the prisoners lined up and shot in the back. Not a one survived."

Jimmy's brow furrowed in thought as he listened.

Slocum continued. "Dunnigan and his men stripped the bodies, took everything of value from those they'd murdered in cold blood, and drifted back into camp, laughing and joking. Even bragging about how he'd killed more than two dozen men himself. Of course, he said it had been in battle—not helpless men with no weapons and with their backs to him."

Slocum could see the questions, the confusion, in the boy's eyes. But Jimmy sat without speaking, listening intently. Slocum's mouth seemed to go dry; it had been a long time since he'd put that many words together all at once. He sipped at his coffee and dragged at the cigarillo, reducing its length by a half inch, his jaw muscles tight.

"Despite the confusion of that battle," Slocum said, "word eventually got around what Dunnigan had done. Both the South's General Beauregard and the North's General Grant were enraged. Orders came from both camps that Dunnigan was to be shot on sight. Don't bother with a court-martial. Just shoot the bastard."

Slocum paused for a moment. Talking about the Shiloh battle brought back too many sharp, painful memories of mangled bodies and blood that turned water holes and mud red. And the smells.

"So they didn't catch him." Jimmy's statement brought Slocum back to the moment.

"No. Somehow Dunnigan found out. He slipped through the pickets of both armies and disappeared. Deserted. A few months later, we began to pick up rumors he was in Missouri, then Arkansas, then Kansas, killing men, women, and children, looting small towns and homesteads. A lot of men, myself included, have been hunting him ever since."

Jimmy took the remaining stub of the candy stick from his mouth. "But there's something I don't understand. In war, isn't the idea to kill the other soldiers?"

Slocum sighed. "It's more complicated than that, Jimmy. Even in a war that brutal, there's a matter of honor, a matter of respect for the other side. Because while they might be the enemy, they were also men. What Dunnigan did at Shiloh tainted the honor of the Confederacy."

"Is that the only reason you've been huntin' him, Slocum?"

"No. It's only part of it. Two of the men he shot at Shiloh were friends of mine. Another was a cousin."

"Oh." Jimmy fell silent for a moment, then asked, "Why'd he do that? Kill prisoners, I mean."

Slocum's jaw joint ached. He realized he had been clenching his teeth. "Because, Jimmy, Dirk Dunnigan is a mean son of a bitch. Mean to the core, a coward, a man with no sense of right and wrong. A cold-blooded killer, pure and simple. The war made some men like that. Dunnigan was just born mean."

Jimmy rose, refilled their coffee cups, and stared into the night. Full darkness had fallen; the brighter stars shone through the thin dust haze above. In the distance an owl sent out a sleepy hoot, receiving a lazy reply. The wind, dying now with the coming of night, ruffled the leaves of the trees.

Finally, Jimmy spat. "When we catch up with them, Slocum, he's all yours. I reckon you deserve it."

Slocum merely nodded. The two finished their coffee in silence, Slocum going through another cigarillo, then spread their bedrolls.

"Slocum?"

"Yes, Jimmy?"

"I—I didn't see it, but I could tell what them men did to Mom. Before they killed her. Do you think they'll do the—the same—to Sissy?"

Slocum decided not to give the boy a straight yes. Jimmy had suffered enough. "If they do, would it make a difference? In the way you feel about her?"

"No, not me. But what would it do to her? Would she be the same Sissy I had before?"

Slocum sighed. "I have no way of knowing, Jimmy." Which was the truth. Some women came away from such experiences with nothing more than a few scars. Others went completely insane. Some fell in between the two extremes. It all depended on the woman. "Better get some sleep now, partner," Slocum said softly. "We've got a long ride ahead of us tomorrow."

Meg Forrest huddled beneath the dirty, thin blanket near the dead ashes of the campfire in the dry, rugged mountains, unable and unwilling to sleep despite the heavy weight of exhaustion.

The coarse rope that bound her wrists and ankles scraped at the chafed skin beneath with each movement; the thin rawhide loop around her throat tightened ever so slightly with each toss and turn of the slightly built man snoring near her side, the free end of the leather thong tied solidly to his left wrist.

For the last three weeks—ever since she'd tried to run the second time—the man called Shiloh, or sometimes Dirk, or Colonel, had bound her hand and foot whenever they camped.

Even during the day, as the horses struggled, lurched, and skidded up one rocky or sandy hill and down another, or splashed hock-deep across creeks and rivers, the leather thong remained about her neck. She would wear a thin scar around her throat the rest of her life. If they let her live at all.

Meg had only a vague notion of where they were or where they were headed. She had gathered from scraps of conversation that the river they generally followed was the Rio Grande, that they were somewhere in southern New Mexico, that the mountains were called the San Andreas, and that two days' ride downriver was the town called Messila. And that they were bound for someplace called Shiloh, like the man beside her, deep in the mountains of Mexico.

She shivered beneath the thin blanket, though the night air was only cool, not bone-biting cold as it had been in the higher mountains to the north.

Meg's body tensed and her breath caught in her throat as the man beside her flopped over, his hand coming to rest on her breast. She steeled herself for the pain of his fingers against the tender flesh, the cruel pinch and twist of her nipple, but it never came. He snored on. Meg knew better than to try to wriggle free of the coarse hand. To wake him would be to invite the brutal squeeze, the twisting fingers. Or worse.

The tension slowly drained from her muscles, replaced by a deep loathing, the revulsion and pure, cold hate she had never before known in her twenty years on this earth. One day, by God, she swore silently, jaws clenched, this bastard will pay for what he's done.

He could never pay enough—

She almost cried out at the sudden cramp low in her abdomen, and felt the ooze of blood into the bundle of rags stuffed between the legs of the dirty, oversized trousers she wore.

For once she welcomed the painful "time of the moon," as her mother had called it. For the first time in her years as a woman, "the curse" brought a double blessing. It meant she hadn't been made pregnant. And that, for a time at least, the men would leave her alone. She wouldn't let herself give in to the deep, gnawing fear of what disease or diseases they might already have given her. Just the thought seemed to set tiny, unseen things to wriggling in her. If she dwelled on it, she thought she could actually feel the diseases working their way up. It was almost too much to bear.

Of all the men in the outlaw band, the woman's curse struck pure terror into one heart.

The full-blood Comanche renegade the other men called Injun Tom, or just Tom, stayed as far from her as possible, would not touch her, or even eat with the group. He made his own meals and ate by himself, well away from the camp. When they did make eye contact, Meg could plainly see the hint of loathing and obvious raw fear in the man's almost black eyes.

When her time finally became too obvious to miss—especially by groping hands—most of the other men sarcastically mocked the Indian as a "superstitious damn redskin." Meg finally understood why, from snippets of conversation overheard. The Comanche might ride with the white outlaws, but his deeply ingrained culture was in the saddle with him. To touch a woman during her time, or come into contact with anything the woman had touched, was the worst possible medicine.

Injun Tom was superstitious about more than just women in their blood time. He rode an albino horse, pure white—big medicine in a war pony. Meg had never seen a pure albino before, and when she first noticed the horse's eyes, glowing red from visible blood vessels, the sight frightened her. It was as if she were looking into the fiery eyes of a devil.

Meg instinctively knew the Comanche was the most dangerous man in camp. His broad, stocky body, bowed legs, and scarred trunk—he usually rode bare from the waist up—rippled with heavy, powerful muscles. The near-ebony eyes in the wide, dark, menacing face were the most frightening thing about him. At first glance they seemed expressionless, but a longer look hinted at a cold cruelty beneath. She knew he would gladly slit her throat in a heartbeat. For now, at least, she was safe from that. He wouldn't touch her.

The others didn't share the same intensity of revulsion and certainly not the terror of the Comanche toward her now. But

even at that they avoided her, as though her blood time made
her unclean.

She welcomed the avoidance.

It gave her time to plan. Twice she had tried to escape, twice
she had failed. It would be more difficult now, bound as she
was, and closely watched. But she would keep trying until she
either succeeded or died.

Meg didn't try to fool herself into thinking she didn't fear
death. She wasn't that strong. She couldn't grab a knife and
plunge the blade into her own heart. That took more courage
than she could find within her.

And there was Jimmy.

For the hundredth time, she thanked God that he had been
away hunting when these men came. If Jimmy had been there,
they would have shot him down just like Father—she forced
away the image that tried to form in her mind, the bullet-
riddled body in the dusty front yard. And the searing memory
of what they had done to her mother, forcing Meg to watch,
before they took their turn with Meg. Then they had killed her
mother. Jimmy had been spared that too.

Meg knew her brother well; they had shared each other's
fears, trust, and secrets since he had been a mere toddler.
Jimmy wasn't quite a man yet, but he was no fool. He would
have found refuge somewhere. Meg knew he wasn't dead. She
did not know how she knew; she just knew. He was out there
somewhere, waiting.

She had to live, to get back to him. It wasn't just that he
needed her, nor she him. They needed each other. When she
got away she would go find him. Try to restart two lives with
his help.

Meg sighed in blessed relief when the man beside her fidgeted again, rolled onto his side away from her, and his hand
moved from her swollen, tender breast. The weight of the hand
had been painful against her raw, chafed nipple and the ach-
ingly full mound beneath.

She glared at the slope-shouldered man snoring beside her.
He was barely as tall as Meg's own five feet two, and probably
didn't outweigh her by much. But he was deceptively strong,
with tiny feet and oversized hands that didn't seem to fit the

rest of his frame. When he was awake, his pale gray eyes glittered in a more frightening cruelty than the Indian's. This man called Shiloh lived to inflict pain. To kill. Meg didn't understand why he was that way. It was enough to know what he was.

Meg shivered again. Shiloh's hand had dragged part of the thin blanket from her shoulders as he rolled over. The chill of the night air deepened. She made no effort to reclaim the covering from him. The cold was nothing compared to the risk of waking him.

She tried to force the physical discomfort from her mind, concentrating on the other men in the outlaw camp, trying to find a weakness in one or the other she might exploit.

None of the men seemed to have much in common.

The big man called Hank snored in his bedroll a few feet away, his six-foot-four frame that carried more than two hundred pounds a hulking dark blob in the faint starlight. It was obvious that he was the number-two man in the outfit behind Shiloh. Hank was a brute of a man, despite his bad leg. His foot angled sharply inward, so much so that he walked almost on the side of his ankle.

It seemed odd to Meg, but Hank had a big, booming laugh that roared from behind tobacco-stained, crooked teeth and ruffled his bushy mustache. His dark brown eyes usually glittered in amusement at one thing or another. Of all the men in camp, Hank was the only one who seemed to have a sense of humor—albeit a crude one. He rode the big, ill-tempered roan with the toed-out foot. Meg knew nothing of the workings of his mind.

Across the way lay the thin form of the one-armed man called Ace, tall, so little meat on his body he was almost a walking skeleton. Meg heard the thin moan from Ace's lips. Her mother had managed to fire one shot from the old cap-and-ball gun before they'd overwhelmed her. That ball had gone through the thin man's side. There was a chance he might yet die from the wound; Meg could only hope he did. A slow and agonizing death.

Meg was more afraid of Ace than she was of the Indian. There was something about him that chilled her blood and made her shiver even on the hottest day.

Joaquin, the half-Mexican, half-Anglo, was the only man who had much of anything to do with Injun Tom. Joaquin often rode alongside the Comanche, the two talking in a curious mix of languages Meg could only assume were Spanish and Comanche. With the other men, Joaquin was as soft-spoken as Hank was garrulous. Meg now knew the swarthy Joaquin had a gift with horses and for reading sign. And that was all she could figure out about him.

The youngest—and most puzzling—one of the bunch was the young man called Brazos.

Under other circumstances, Meg knew, she might be drawn to him. His face was tanned by sun and wind, but still unlined and handsome; she guessed his age at somewhere in the mid-twenties. He was of medium height, with wavy, dark brown hair that almost touched gently sloping shoulders, narrow hips, long legs, and a fluid way of moving that reminded Meg of the controlled gait of a blooded horse, a quickness of muscle always under firm control, yet ready to explode into action in a heartbeat. He was clean, almost dapper even through the trail dust, and the only one who bathed and shaved at every opportunity.

And he was the only man who hadn't raped her.

Told it was his turn, he had barely glanced at Meg, with a strange expression in his odd amber eyes. That look haunted Meg. His eyes held no sign of lust or want. Nor was it an expression of pity; more a look of revulsion, if anything. He quickly shifted his gaze from her, shook his head, and strode away.

On the trail, Brazos had been the only man to show her any consideration, any sign that she was more than a body to be used. When he filled her plate, she had enough to fill her belly. That wasn't the case with Shiloh or the others. At times, she caught a quick glimpse of Brazos's gaze on her, but couldn't read his thoughts. He seldom spoke, content to acknowledge Shiloh's or Hank's instructions with a silent nod.

He hadn't taken her mother either—

Meg's breath caught in her throat as a shadowy form loomed over her. A moment later, a second blanket settled across her body. She nodded her thanks, but didn't know if

Brazos saw. The shadow disappeared as quickly as it materialized, without a sound.

She was sure of only one thing.

Brazos didn't fit in here. Maybe, she thought, Brazos could be used. Even as the idea formed in her mind, reality brought the sting of tears of frustration and despair to her lids.

She didn't know how to use men.

Until these outlaws came, she had been a virgin.

Still, there had to be a way. If there was a God above, there would be a way. She closed her eyes and sent a silent message into the night sky:

Hang on, Jimmy. I'll be back. I promise. . . .

5

Slocum racked the brass ladder of the tang sight on the Peabody up to the three-hundred-yard mark, thumbed the heavy side-hammer to full cock, and settled his elbows into the slight depressions that served as his rifle pit on the rim of the steep canyon wall.

The range wasn't quite four hundred yards, and downhill. Slocum made the mental calculations without conscious thought, corrected his hold, and squeezed the trigger.

The Peabody laid a generous thump into his shoulder and loosed a cloud of blue-gray powder smoke. An instant after the muzzle blast jarred his eardrums, he heard the faint but distinctive thump of lead into flesh. Slocum racked the action, extracted the spent brass, and reloaded as the light breeze carried away the obscuring gun smoke.

He didn't cock the hammer. There was no need for a second shot. The young bull elk took a couple of faltering strides, sank to its front knees, then toppled onto its side on the grassy bank of the stream below.

Slocum glanced over his shoulder and nodded in satisfaction. The heavy muzzle blast had startled the horses a bit, but Jimmy easily kept them under control. Slocum waited another minute, just to make sure the elk stayed down, then rose, shouldered the rifle, and strode back to the horses.

"Get him?" Jimmy asked.

"Yes. He's down." Slocum slid the Peabody back into its boot on the near side-pommel of his saddle. "Mount up, Jimmy. The quicker we get him field dressed, the better the meat."

The boy nodded silently and toed the stirrup. Slocum led the way down the canyon wall, letting his trail-savvy bay set his own pace along the narrow, twisting game trail. Jimmy held his sorrel a good dozen yards behind Slocum, the roan packhorse trailing on loose lead.

Slocum reined in near the downed elk, satisfied. The heavy Peabody slug had taken the animal exactly where Slocum intended, shattering the heart and ripping through both lungs. The animal hadn't suffered. It had been dead on its feet from the time the bullet hit.

Jimmy sat the saddle beside Slocum, staring at the dead elk, his eyes wide. "I never seen a real elk before. Just pictures in a book we used to have. They're big."

Slocum dismounted and pulled his skinning knife from its belt sheath. "This is a young one. Only six, maybe seven hundred pounds. On older bulls, the meat's tougher. Young cow elk's the best of all," Slocum said as he worked.

Jimmy swung down and watched. The boy obviously had no idea how to go about field dressing an elk, but he could learn almost as much by watching as by doing.

"Thought elk was mountain animals," Jimmy said. "How come there's one this far south, no mountains around?"

"There used to be a lot of them on the South Plains range, along with buffalo, mountain lion, bear, and the big gray wolves mostly associated with the high country. There are still a few of each around. Not as many as before the buffalo hunters came, but you'll run across a handful now and then."

Jimmy fell silent for a moment, then said, "Slocum, I got to ask. How come you shot this one? We don't need the meat."

Slocum wiped his knife blade clean and stood. "We don't. But they do."

"They?"

Slocum nodded toward the bend in the canyon upstream, to the northeast. He heard Jimmy's breath catch in his throat and glanced at the boy. His eyes had gone even wider, his face a touch whiter.

The horsemen sat astride a couple of hundred yards away, dark men on tough, rangy horses.

"My God!" Jimmy half gasped, startled. "Injuns!"

"Quahadi Comanches, to be specific," Slocum said calmly.

"What—where—God, there's five of 'em—"

"Eight. They always try to form parties in groups of four. It's their medicine number. One is on the west side of the canyon rim, another on the east, and one trailing the rest of them by half a mile to make sure nobody comes up behind them. They've been watching us for most of the day."

Jimmy's gaze flicked to one canyon wall, then the other. "But I never seen 'em—why didn't you tell me, Slocum?"

Slocum shrugged. "Thought you'd learn more this way. Like to always keep an eye and ear cocked, even when you think you're the only living soul for miles. When a Comanche doesn't want to be seen, he's hard to spot."

"You seen 'em."

"That's one reason I've stayed alive this long."

The boy's muscles tensed as the horsemen moved toward them, their mounts at a slow walk. A stocky man, thick of shoulder and whose head seemed overly large even for his muscled body, led the way, mounted on a dappled gray mustang.

"What do we do now, Slocum? Run or fight?" Jimmy's hand dropped to the stock of the .38-40 in its rifle boot.

"Neither. These men aren't likely to take our scalps. It's a scouting party, not a war party."

"How do you know that?"

"No women and children along, for one thing. And they're not painted for war." Slocum cut a reassuring glance Jimmy's way. "Besides, I know the one out front. Just don't try to pull a weapon and we won't have any trouble."

The barrel-chested rider on the gray drew his mount to a stop a few feet from Slocum. There was no visible expression on the wide, scarred face the color of deeply burnished copper, or in the black eyes. The breeze ruffled the long mane and tail of the gray horse.

Jimmy thought his heart was going to burst from pounding in fright. He'd never seen a real, live Indian before. These men didn't look like the drawings he'd seen in the books; in the pictures they had been all but naked, paint streaked over their bodies, long feathered headdresses flowing in the wind.

Two of them wore white man's clothes, even stockman's-style hats with flat crowns and floppy brims. The others wore woven-cloth or animal-skin shirts and breeches. Each wore a single braid of long, dark hair that fell down his shoulders past his chest, the ends of the twist tied off with a bit of colored cloth. All wore moccasins similar to those in Slocum's trail pack. And they were well armed. All but one carried rifles, the long guns ranging from old percussion muskets to the stocky man's new repeating Winchester. Big knives rested in sheaths at their waists.

The one who didn't carry a gun had a short bow slung over his back. The feathered tips of a quiver of arrows showed over his shoulder and a short-handled axe nestled against his side. That one wore a headband, a strip of faded yellow and red cloth with a single dark feather tucked beneath it and lying against his neck and upper shoulder.

Jimmy swallowed hard, trying to check the tingle in his spine. These Indians, up close and alive, were more scary than the drawings in the books.

It was the eyes that made them spooky. The expressions reflected there ranged from glints of hate—in the man with the headband—to blank indifference to the faint hint of warmth in the gaze of the man out front, who Jimmy instinctively sensed was the leader of the band.

The stocky Indian stared directly at Jimmy for what seemed to be a long time, then shifted his gaze back to Slocum and rattled off some words in a deep, growling language Jimmy didn't recognize. Slocum growled something back, then gestured toward the dead elk. The Indian turned to his companions and said a few words; within moments, three of the men knelt beside the elk carcass, knives flashing. A short time later, three more Indians rode up, converging from different directions. The stocky man had dismounted and now squatted on his heels before Slocum, who immediately lowered himself into a similar position.

Jimmy knew now that if Slocum was wrong about these men, the two of them were dead. Against eight Indians they wouldn't stand a chance if it came to a fight. He tried not to think about it.

When the swarthy Indian facing Slocum abruptly switched to English, Jimmy all but jumped in surprise.

"Good to see you, Slocum. Long time," he said.

"Nine, ten winters," Slocum said casually. "How goes the hunt, Night Crawler?"

The Indian grimaced. "Not as in our younger days, Slocum. The buffalo grow scarce, the elk and bear harder to find. White-man cows fill the belly, but not the spirit. How goes the hunt with you?"

It was Slocum's turn to frown. "The trail we follow is old, my friend." Slocum gestured toward Jimmy. "My partner, Jimmy Forrest."

A quick gaze from obsidian eyes flicked to Jimmy, then back to Slocum. Jimmy lost track of the conversation then as the two men slipped into a strange mix of languages that Jimmy finally guessed were Comanche, Spanish, and some other tongue he had never heard before, with an occasional word in English.

He turned his attention to the Comanches working on the elk. Already, they had the skin removed and the animal gutted. The man with the headband—he seemed young when compared to the others—chewed on a chunk of raw liver, blood smearing his lips and dripping from his chin.

Jimmy checked the urge to edge back as the Comanche rose from his squat, strode to him, and held out a bloody hand clutching a chunk of raw elk liver. Jimmy managed to suppress the sudden churn of his belly. He hated liver, even cooked.

"No, thanks," Jimmy said.

The Comanche looked puzzled; Jimmy realized the man didn't understand English. Jimmy forced a smile, shook his head, patted his right hand on his stomach, and faked a belch.

A faint smile touched the Indian's lips. He nodded in understanding at the universal sign for "full belly," then turned back to the other Comanches. One had stripped a portion of intestine between his fingers and chewed enthusiastically on the gut; the other gnawed on a mouthful of liver.

Jimmy had heard Indians referred to as "red savages," and watching them chew on the elk's guts, he thought maybe the term fit. It sure fit their dinner habits anyway.

The young brave with the headband carved two more chunks from the liver and carried the gory meat to Slocum and Night Crawler. The Comanche and Slocum took the meat and chewed on it as they talked; when it was gone, Slocum pulled two of his prized cigarillos from his pocket, handed one to the Comanche, and lit both smokes. Jimmy began to feel more comfortable. He had heard that when a white man and an Indian smoked together, no harm was likely to come to either. He hoped the story was true.

Jimmy picked up a few English words from the jumbled conversation. The word "Shiloh" was mentioned several times.

The parley dragged on for quite some time before Slocum and Night Crawler stood and shook hands, white-man style.

Slocum walked up, retrieved the bay's reins from Jimmy's grip, and mounted. "Interesting parley," Slocum said. "It's time we moved on." He kneed the bay around and led off at an easy, shambling walk.

Jimmy checked the urge to blurt out the dozens of questions that swirled in his mind. The cold knot of fear in his belly slowly warmed as they rode, leaving the canyon and heading south by southwest across a wide sea of parched grass waving in the breeze. They covered about three miles before Jimmy clucked the sorrel up to Slocum's left. He couldn't hold the questions any longer.

"Slocum, were those really wild Indians? I mean, not the reservation kind? I thought all Indians had given up."

"Not that band, along with several others. Many of the Quahadis never signed the treaty papers. That group was, in fact, what you call wild Indians. For all practical purposes, this is still their country. I doubt they'll be able to hold it much longer."

"What if you hadn't known him?"

Slocum shrugged. "Perhaps nothing. Most likely, though, some men would have died. Maybe us."

Jimmy's mind chewed on that nervous idea for a quarter of a mile. But he had learned something. His gaze flicked constantly around the countryside now, and occasionally he twisted in the saddle to study their backtrail.

"Take it easy, Jimmy," Slocum finally said. "They won't follow us."

"You sure you can trust that Injun?"

"As much as I trust any man."

"Funny name, Night Crawler. Why would he be named after a worm?"

Slocum chuckled. "He wasn't. Night Crawler is sort of a nickname. Basically, it means he was a great lover in his younger days. A complimentary nickname." Slocum lit another cigarillo, pinched the match head between his fingers, broke the stem, and put the pieces of the lucifer back in his shirt pocket. "Among the Comanche, night crawling is part of their culture. When a girl wants to share a man's bed and he has given some sign he wants her, she just crawls under the edge of his lodge, slips under his blankets, then sneaks out again before daylight."

Slocum dragged at his smoke and cut a quick smile at Jimmy. "It's said among the Quahadi that if any eligible woman, young or old, missed a visit to Night Crawler, it was because she was excessively ugly or didn't know he was in camp."

"Oh." Jimmy's face warmed.

"His tribal name is more descriptive of the real man," Slocum said. "It's Ute Killer. He's one of the most respected warriors in the entire Comanche nation. The Comanches and Utes have been mortal enemies for longer than anyone in either tribe can remember. The Utes, in fact, gave the Comanches their name. In Ute, it's *Komantica,* or 'enemy.'"

"He didn't look so tough," Jimmy said.

"Never judge a man's fighting ability, or his heart, by the way he looks, Jimmy."

"How come you know each other?"

Slocum chuckled. "We met through a sort of contest. He stole some horses from me—the Comanches take great pride in their ability as horse thieves—and I stole them back. He stole them again, I stole them back again. That went on for most of two months before the two of us decided to meet and call it off, to recognize we were equals in the horse-thief game." He tapped a bit of ash from the cigarillo. "Being an honored horse thief saved my scalp a couple of times in Comanche country."

Slocum paused for a breath, wondering what it was about this boy riding beside him that made him spout out more words at one time than he ever could with grown men. He quit fretting on it and turned his mind to the job ahead.

After a half mile or so, Slocum said, "Jimmy, what I learned from Night Crawler means we've got a decision to make."

Jimmy's thin eyebrows went up. "What's that?"

"Night Crawler knows of the men we're hunting."

"He knows them?" Eagerness flashed into the boy's words.

"Not personally. But he knows *of* them. Night Crawler's band covers a lot of country in the course of a year, from near Canada to deep into Mexico. The Indian grapevine is just as quick, and for the most part more accurate than the white man's telegraph. He said he has a pretty good idea where we can find Shiloh Dunnigan."

Jimmy's grip on the reins tightened. "Where?"

"The Sierra Madre Mountains, deep in Sonora, Mexico. Dunnigan has a stronghold there, a small town he and his men took over from the Mexican peasants. He renamed it Shiloh, after himself. What Dub Packer told me jibes with what Night Crawler said. Dunnigan's on his way there."

Jimmy's jaw muscles clenched, his fear over the encounter with the Comanches now far from his mind. "How far?"

"A long way," Slocum said calmly. "We could save several days' ride if we take a risk. We'd have to go into and across the Devil's Hole country."

"Devil's Hole?"

Slocum nodded. "It's one of most dangerous places between Canada and South America, Jimmy. Almost five hun-

dred square miles of bandits, robbers, and killers—red, white,
and brown—who would kill a man just to watch him kick.
Riding into Devil's Hole would be taking a big gamble.''

A muscle knotted in Jimmy's jaw. ''It's worth a try.''

Slocum said, ''Even at that, we couldn't reach Shiloh before
Dunnigan and his men do. I won't lie to you. Getting your
sister out of that stronghold is going to be a tough chore, and
we can't help her if we get killed on the way.''

Jimmy squinted into the distance for a moment, teeth
clenched, thinking. He turned to Slocum. ''Every day they've
got her is misery, Slocum. For me, but I'm afraid mostly for
her. Let's go the short way.''

Slocum nodded. ''I figured you'd say that. I would have, in
your place.''

Silence fell for another mile or so before Jimmy again
turned to face Slocum. ''There's something ain't neither of us
said yet, Slocum, but it's got to be said. *If* she's still alive.''

''Yes, Jimmy. If she's still alive. . . .''

Meg Forrest had lost track of the days.

They seemed to run one into the other, a blur of passing
mountains and streams and stretches of dry desert and grassy
plains and long hours astride the spiny backbone of the old
paint mare. Nights when she dared not fall asleep until the
demands of her muscles overpowered the fear of her mind.

She didn't know if two weeks or three had passed since that
terrible day on the Republican River, so many painful miles
behind in distance, but only a nightmare away when she could
no longer hold her eyes open.

Meg realized with a start she had dozed off on the old
mare's back. The thought set her heart pounding. A fall would
snap the noose painfully tight against her neck, and bring a
curse—or a cruel laugh—from the small man riding in front
of her, holding the free end of the rawhide reata. She willed
her eyes open despite the scratchy, sand-like rasp of her eye-
lids each time she blinked.

The aching heaviness of muscle and sluggishness of mind
were not Meg's major torment.

It was the filth.

Days had passed since she'd last had the opportunity to even wash, let alone bathe. Her own body odor sent ripples of revulsion through her brain. Sweat-caked dirt and sand soiled every wrinkle of her skin and the filthy clothing she wore. Her shoulder-length hair, once golden, now fell stiff, heavy, and dark. Her scalp itched constantly, as if attacked by the same squirmy things that seemed to wriggle deeper into her body from her crotch.

She thought with longing of the almost daily baths, the clean smell of freshly laundered cloth that had been part of her life until these men came. And if she didn't get a long bath and chance to wash her clothing soon, she feared she would go mad.

But she would ask no favors of the man called Shiloh.

At least now the going was easier along the banks of the stream the men called the Rio Bravo, or sometimes the Rio Grande. The old mare's sharp backbone was less painful to Meg now. Three days' ride from the Republican, the young man named Brazos had fashioned an Indian-style saddle for her, a couple of worn blankets draped across a thick horsehair pad and buckled into place by a single band of leather the width of her hand.

It wasn't much and it lacked the support and comfort of stirrups, but compared to riding bareback, it was as near to luxury as she had known since the outlaws had come.

The man called Shiloh swiveled his head, studying the lay of the land along the riverbank, then reined his horse into the mouth of a narrow side canyon.

Meg glanced over her shoulder at the riders who followed. Hank and Ace rode stirrup to stirrup, Hank talking as usual, the skeletal Ace with the elbow of his one arm pressed against his side. Injun Joe and Joaquin also rode together, occasionally trading comments, Joaquin jovial, the Comanche in his normal surly state aboard the scary-looking albino horse.

Brazos trailed a few yards behind, ever the loner, speaking only when he had to, his face still an unreadable mask. Yet he was the only one of the group to show a spark of compassion toward Meg.

Despite the circumstances and the grinding weight of fear and exhaustion, Meg found herself intrigued by the young man. Whether it was because of the small favors he had done her, or that he alone had touched neither her nor her mother, or perhaps a sense that he was the weak link in the chain of the band and could somehow be used, she didn't know. But there was something about him—

Her musings stopped abruptly as Shiloh pulled his horse to a stop beside the high north wall of the canyon. A spring burbled from the rocky, almost vertical stone bluff, feeding a series of pools that threaded through a stand of juniper and pinyon pine and tangles of huisache and berry vines on its way to the river beyond. A grassy meadow nourished by the stream and dotted with cactus and the spiny plant called Spanish dagger spread from the timber and brush out across the canyon floor.

"This will do," Shiloh said as the others rode up. "It's the best camp we'll find along the Rio, and half a day's ride to Mesilla. All right, set to—and make it a good camp, one for three, four days."

The sun was only halfway down the western sky when the camp was ready and a sparse meal prepared and eaten. Shiloh put his plate aside and rose.

"Hank, Ace, Joaquin, saddle up. Bring a packhorse. We're going into Mesilla, get resupplied, and have the sawbones there take a look at that little hole in Ace's side. Tom, you and Brazos stay here. Mind the horses and the girl. You know what to do if she tries to run off again." He tossed the free end of the reata to Brazos.

Brazos merely nodded, but the Comanche cut a quick, bright glance at Meg and seemed to recoil slightly. She caught the lingering look of fear in Joe's obsidian eyes. The terror of menstruating women must run deep in Comanche men, she thought; her last flow had been three days ago, but she pretended her time of month lingered. At least it kept Shiloh and the others at bay. For now.

She busied herself cleaning up the utensils from the quick meal, interrupting her chores to watch as the four horsemen rounded the mouth of the canyon and disappeared from view.

Brazos held the end of the reata loosely, careful to give her plenty of slack, and when Shiloh and the others rode from sight, he tucked the rawhide casually beneath the belt of his leather shotgun-style chaps and helped Meg finish up.

With the last fry pan stowed, Meg said her thanks to Brazos for his help. The two sat side by side on a fallen tree trunk near the fire. Meg glanced around.

"Where's Tom?" she asked.

Brazos nodded toward the steep bluff that towered overhead. "Up top, I expect. Standing watch. Not that it's necessary. Mostly, it's just a chance for him to get off by himself. He's not much for company."

The length of Brazos's statement startled Meg a bit; it was more words than she'd heard him say all the way from Nebraska. His voice was neither deep nor tenor, but pleasant to the ear. Meg sensed she would never have a better chance to draw the young man out, to try to find what went on behind those hazel eyes.

"Brazos, you're the only man here who has shown me any courtesy." She chanced reaching out to place a hand on his forearm, felt the sudden tension in the muscles beneath her touch, and quickly let the hand drop away. "I just want you to know I appreciate it."

He answered only with a nod, his gaze not meeting hers. After a moment, he rolled and lit a cigarette. A quarter of the smoke was ashes before he suddenly spoke.

"Miss, I'm sorry. For what happened to your folks. And to you. But I couldn't have stopped them. Not when they were liquored up and kill-crazy like that . . ."

"I know, Brazos. I also know you didn't fire a shot, you didn't—didn't touch my mother—or me. It's them I hate. Not you." She waited for a response, not really expecting one. When none came, she drew a deep breath and decided to push her luck. "Why are you here, Brazos? With this bunch? You're no outlaw."

For the first time, his expression changed. The wide-set amber eyes in his tanned face narrowed, a muscle twitched in his jaw, and his free hand curled into a fist. Still, he didn't speak until he finished his cigarette and ground it beneath his boot heel. He didn't look at Meg, but kept his gaze focused somewhere beyond the camp.

"Yes, I am an outlaw. I killed two people back in Ohio."

"Then there must have been a reason."

"Not when it's the one crime beyond imagination. The two people I killed were my parents."

Meg's breath caught in her throat; her skin turned cold.

"But—why?"

He finally turned to face her, his jaw set in defiance, or possibly anger; for a moment, Meg feared he was going to strike her. But the fear faded when she looked into the gold-flecked, hazel eyes and saw the inner pain and torment reflected there. "Why do you want to know?" he demanded. "What business is it of yours?"

Meg ignored the sudden sharp, suspicious tone to his words. "Because I care."

"Why should you? Nobody else does."

Meg sighed. Her shoulders slumped. "It would help me understand why you're different from the others. Why I have this feeling we're both captives here. Granted, your personal life is none of my business. Of course, if you don't want to talk about it, I understand."

The tension slowly drained from his features, but the haunted look remained in his eyes. He studied her for a long time. "I never told anybody about it."

"Maybe it would help if you did. Keeping something like that bottled up inside just adds more hurt. For what it's worth, I'll not tell anyone else. It will go no farther than my ears. I just don't believe you—unlike these others—would kill without justification."

Brazos studied her again for several heartbeats, doubt, pain, and the need to talk clearly warring in his eyes. Then he cleared his throat. "You won't believe. Nobody would believe. It's not a pretty story."

Meg studied the haunted look in his eyes for a moment. Instinct told her Brazos truly wanted—needed—to tell someone. She nodded. "If you want to tell me."

The young man looked away again, unable or unwilling to meet Meg's gaze. He sighed heavily. His shoulders slumped.

He shifted his gaze from her face and sat staring into the distance.

"Father raped my little sister. Mother held her down while he did it. I saw the whole thing."

Meg's hand went to her mouth in shock. "Oh, my God," she half whispered. "What kind of animal—animals—could do that?"

"Fine, upstanding, churchgoing pillars of the community, that's what kind." The bitterness and hate tightened Brazos's words. "We lived in a small house on the outskirts of a little town a few miles from Springfield. Mother was a schoolteacher, Father a bookkeeper. They were always in the second pew on Sunday mornings and Wednesday evenings, always had a folded bill, not just a few coins, for the collection plate. Until that one summer day, I didn't know the truth for certain myself."

He reached for the makings and rolled another cigarette. "They weren't nice people at all, miss," he said after lighting his smoke. "It's a long story. The short version is, the day it happened I was in the barn mending some harness when I heard Allie scream loud, like she was really hurt, but it was a short cry, sort of cut off right in the middle."

He worked the cigarette for a moment, still staring away from Meg, unwilling to meet her gaze. "For some reason I didn't just go charging up to the house to see what happened. It was summer. The window of Allie's room was open. When I slipped up to the side of the house, I could see in. Father was"—his voice caught a bit—"doing it to Allie. Mother had one hand on her shoulder, holding her down, the other over her mouth. I heard her say several times, 'see what happens to bad little girls who sass their parents?' "

"My God," Meg said softly through the horror that tightened her throat, "their own daughter—how could they—"

Brazos finally turned to look at Meg. The cold, hard glitter in his eyes contrasted sharply with what seemed to be tears pooled in his lower lids. "I should have seen it coming," he said, "but I was just thirteen." Near Jimmy's age, Meg thought. "I should have known by the way they punished her, which had become more and more often in the last few months before it happened.''

He crushed the cigarette and rolled another. "Father would bend Allie over his lap, and Mother would flip her dress up and pull down her underpants. Father would spank her hard, but it seemed like he would leave his hand on her bottom a long time before the next blow. When it was over, he and Mother would be breathing hard. They'd go into their bedroom and shut the door. I could hear . . . things going on in there while I tried to help Allie." He paused to light the cigarette.

"I should have known, and that made it my fault too, because maybe I could have done what I did sooner and it would never have happened. But I was too young to understand at the time. The day it finally happened was Allie's birthday. She was ten years old."

Meg finally trusted her voice enough to speak. "What a horrible, horrible thing. You weren't to blame, Brazos. You didn't know."

He sighed heavily. "I knew what to do then. When they got dressed to go to church—it was a Wednesday, which was prayer-meeting night—I stayed behind. They left Allie where she was, all bloody between the legs. She didn't cry. Didn't make a sound. Just stared up at the ceiling. And the look in her eyes scared me. It was like she didn't live behind them anymore. She never said a word that day. Or ever again."

Brazos paused to finish his cigarette, squinting through the smoke, still not looking at Meg.

"Please—go on. What happened then?"

"I cleaned Allie up as best I could, got her dressed, gathered up some clothes for both of us, what money I could find, anything we could eat, and hitched up the mare to the old buckboard." Brazos's tone chilled and tightened. "I took Father's old shotgun out of the closet, sat down in a chair, and waited. When they got back from church, I killed them both. I put Allie in the buckboard seat beside me. We left Ohio that night. I've been running ever since."

Meg sat quietly for a moment, trying to push away the image that formed in her mind of the young girl on the bed, trying to comprehend how anyone, especially a mother and father, could do that to a helpless child. Compared to what Allie had been through, Meg's own horrors amounted to little. Her heart went out to the little girl. And to the man who sat beside her.

"Couldn't you have gone to the authorities? Told them why you had done what you had done?"

Finally, he turned to look at Meg. The haunted look in his eyes cut into her. "They wouldn't have believed me. No one would have. Who would take the word of a thirteen-year-old boy who had just killed his own parents? Two of the finest, most God-fearing people in Ohio?" He shook his head. "No one. Not a soul."

"I believe you, Brazos."

"You didn't know them. Or what they seemed to be."

Meg put a hand on his forearm. He didn't flinch from her touch this time. "What happened to her? Allie?"

Brazos hesitated a moment, then sighed. "I failed her again. I had intended to take care of Allie the rest of her life. But we ran out of money in St. Louis. We were hungry, had no place to stay. There was no work to be had. I had to leave her in an orphanage there. I stole a saddle, mounted the buggy mare, and headed west. A year later, I sent a telegram to the orphanage, asking about her. They wired back that she had been dead for six months."

After a moment, Meg cleared her throat. "I think I can understand what a terrible loss that was for you. There's a special bond between brothers and sisters—" She caught herself; these men didn't know about Jimmy. It was best that way. "Or so I've heard," she finished a bit lamely.

Brazos shook his head. "I've thought about asking what happened to her, but can't take the chance. Some things I don't want to know."

Meg gave his forearm a slight squeeze, then dropped her hand away. "I understand."

The steely look reappeared in his amber eyes. "I've talked too much, and I'm not sure why. I'll hold you to your word not tell this to anyone else."

"I won't."

"And don't think this means I will, or can, help you. At least not now. If I tried, Shiloh would kill me, slowly. What they would do to you would be worse."

"Could they do anything worse than what they've already done?"

"Yes, they could. Believe me. I've seen it."

The cold, flat tone of his voice brought an inward shudder to Meg. Brazos abruptly stood and strode away, leaving Meg alone on the fallen tree trunk. He stopped at the far edge of the camp, staring into the distance. The end of the rawhide thong around Meg's neck lay beside her on the ground.

She saw the chance to escape, and at the same time the futility of trying. Brazos might not know she had slipped away until it was too late. But the Comanche would. She felt the weight from the stare of black eyes on her, though she couldn't see Injun Tom. He was out there. The Indian wouldn't touch her. He wouldn't have to. A bullet could do it for him and save his medicine at the same time.

Her spirits sank at the idea of freedom from these men, freedom so near and yet so far beyond her reach.

But, she thought, what was it Brazos had said? That he couldn't help her "at least not now." Would the time ever come?

She didn't know. All she could do was hope to stay alive until she got the answer.

6

Jimmy knelt beside the narrow, twisting trickle of deceptive stream that looped in lazy near-circles, often twisting back upon itself until it flowed in the opposite direction, as if it had no idea where it was going, before it finally reached the river far to the north.

Here, it had horseshoed aimlessly again, in a near-circle more than a mile long, the slight current drifting away toward the south.

The water looked cool and clean, but it was warm—almost hot—to the touch. Despite its sparkling clarity, it was sour on the tongue. But it would do for washing, if not for drinking. The horses hadn't seemed to mind the taste of bad water. Among many things he had learned from Slocum was that animals' systems could handle mineral-laden water that would go through a human like a dose of salts and leave him trotting into the brush so often it was hardly worth mounting between bouts of yanking his trousers down. Jimmy had learned to smell and taste before he drank, no matter how great his thirst.

Beads of moisture still dripped from Jimmy's chin. He wondered idly how a hot desert wind playing against warm water could be cooling to the skin. He would ask Slocum someday. Today it didn't seem important. It was enough that it did.

Jimmy settled back, his buttocks resting on his heels, and studied Slocum, who sat cross-legged in the sparse shade of a twisted mesquite bush, honing the blade of his skinning knife.

Slocum had washed and shaved within an hour of reaching the stream, watering the horses, and setting up a rough semblance of a camp. Jimmy understood the washing. Trail dirt and dust itched the skin, worked its way into a man's clothes until it grated against his skin. He still wasn't sure why a man would go to the trouble to shave out here in the middle of nowhere.

He idly rubbed his own chin. His fingers touched the soft hairs, little more than fuzz, but which now seemed more plentiful and a bit thicker and stiffer. Jimmy also had noticed that the hair at his crotch now was darker, thicker, and coarser. Sometimes he wakened with a tingling ache between his legs and a somewhat embarrassing erection that made it difficult to empty his bladder. If Slocum noticed Jimmy's condition at those times, he said nothing.

Despite the often meager camp fare, Jimmy knew he had fleshed out, put on muscle in the days since they'd left Jacksboro. The clothes he had worn a few short months ago were useless now. He had outgrown them, seemingly overnight. His current outfit and the spare clothing in his saddlebags, bought in the town outside Fort Concho, were a full size too large. But he knew it wouldn't be long until they fit. He still had a way to go, but he was growing into a man, his shoulders and leg muscles thickening by the day. He suspected he might be as tall now as Meg.

The thought of her turned Jimmy's mind from himself, renewing the cold determination in his gut. He sensed that she was closer now, though still far away; the shortcut through Devil's Hole had brought them closer, so far without incident.

Three days ago he had first seen the blue mountains. They'd seemed little more than a few hours' ride at the time, but in those three days it seemed he and Slocum had gotten no closer to the Sierra Madres.

Distances and constant, shimmering heat waves fooled the eye in this dry, barren country where nothing seemed to thrive except rattlesnakes, scorpions, lizards, cactus, and other plants and bushes Jimmy had never before seen. But they were closer to Meg. He felt it. It was enough.

Jimmy leaned forward again, cupped water in his hands, and was about to splash it onto his skin when the hairs at the back of his neck tingled. A thin wisp of sand drifted past on the bottom of the creek. The wisp thickened and became a tannish red streak through the clear water.

"Slocum," Jimmy called softly, "the water. There's mud in it." He had enough trail savvy now to know there was only one way it could have gotten there. Something—animal or man—had crossed upstream, stirring the soil.

Slocum instantly came to his feet, sheathing the knife and grabbing the Winchester that was never more than an arm's length away. Jimmy quickly wiped his wet hands on his shirt, picked up his own rifle, and followed as Slocum picked his way up the rocky slope of the low but steep hill overlooking camp.

"How much mud?" Slocum asked calmly as Jimmy stretched out beside him, just beneath the crown of the hill, high enough that they could see over it but not be easily spotted against the brassy sky.

"Enough it couldn't have been a deer. It'd take a bunch of horses to raise that much."

Slocum nodded, his gaze raking the broken, craggy desert hills to the north.

Jimmy spotted the riders a second after Slocum saw them, dark figures shimmering through heat waves just over a mile away. Headed straight toward them.

"I don't think these are your friends from back yonder, Slocum," Jimmy said.

"They're not." Slocum's tone turned tight. "They're Apaches. Chiricahuas. The last tribe any sane man wants to tangle with. And a full-blown war party to boot, looking for scalps, horses, loot, and prisoners. Mostly scalps."

Jimmy swallowed hard, trying to suppress the growing knot of fear in his gut. "How can you tell?"

"By the way they sit a horse, and the numbers. There's more than twenty of them. It appears we could be in a spot of trouble here."

"What do we do, Slocum? Run?"

Slocum's eyes narrowed. "That would be my preference, but we can't. Our horses are worn down from the miles and lack of grass. We can't outrun them. They'd catch us inside of five miles." He cut a quick glance at Jimmy. "Remember once I mentioned there was a time to run and a time to fight? This is one of those times we fight. Because we have no choice."

"Maybe they won't see us." Jimmy had trouble getting the words out. His mouth had dried up.

"Maybe. But don't count on it. An Apache doesn't miss much. At least they don't yet know we're here."

"How do you know?"

"Because we'd never have seen them if they *did* know. And we'd wake up tomorrow morning with our throats slit."

Jimmy's blood chilled despite the broiling sun directly overhead. The receiver of the .38-40 rifle was slick beneath his hand. "Where do we make our stand?"

"Right here. We've got the high ground. That will be an advantage. Or at least as much of an advantage as a man can have going up against Chiricahuas. We don't have much time to get ready. Let's move."

Jimmy cast one quick glance toward the approaching horsemen before scrambling back down the hill, following Slocum's lead. The Apaches were less than a mile away now, still headed straight toward Slocum and Jimmy.

Within minutes the two had moved the horses deep into the mesquite thicket at the base of the hill, tied them securely with slip knots, and tightened the saddle and pack cinches. "I'll bring my big rifle and saddlebags, Jimmy," Slocum said. He plucked a long horsehair from each of the animals' tails and tied it loosely over their muzzles to keep them from nickering a greeting to the Apaches' ponies. "Bring all the water we have, the canteens and buffalo belly bag."

Jimmy struggled back to the crest of the rocky hill, the weight of the canteens and buffalo gut bag trying to drag him back downslope, his .38-40 rifle and the little .22 Remington both in his free hand.

He sank down beside Slocum, partly out of breath. He glanced up briefly; the Indians were closing now, a bit less than a half mile off. He slipped the .41 Colt Lightning from his belt holster and fumbled a sixth round into the chamber he normally carried empty beneath the hammer.

Slocum already had retrieved his second Peacemaker from the saddlebag, loaded the sixth cylinder of both his handguns, and placed a half dozen of the odd-shaped Peabody cartridges on a flat rock beside the forestock of the big rifle, within easy reloading reach. His .44-40 Winchester lay across his jacket, which was folded on the rock he would use as a shooting rest.

"What—do we—do now, Slocum?" Jimmy gasped, short of breath from the steep climb.

Slocum cracked the actions of the single-shot Peabody and the Winchester to reassure himself a round was chambered in each weapon. "We wait."

Jimmy's heart hammered against his ribs, and not just from the exertion. "Will they charge us? We can't stop that many horses."

Slocum shook his head. "Comanches fight from horseback. Apaches dismount, scatter, and fight on foot. If it comes to shooting, targets will be hard to come by. A Chiricahua can take cover behind a buffalo chip. Should it come to that, make sure you have a good, clear shot before you pull the trigger. Take a good look, Jimmy. How many of them have rifles?"

Jimmy squinted through the heat waves. "Most all of them. I count only three bows."

"That's my count. It puts us up against a lot of rifles. Don't give *them* a clear shot. Chiricahuas can shoot better than most white men. They don't ride the war path for glory and honor. They ride it to kill." He glanced at Jimmy. The boy's face had paled beneath his deepening tan. "Scared, partner?"

"Real scared. You?"

"Any smart man would be, Jimmy." Slocum sure didn't sound scared, Jimmy thought; just calm and collected, as if he didn't have any nerves at all. "Don't start shooting. Maybe they'll just ride on past. Until we have some sign one way or the other, we wait—and keep quiet."

"Could be they don't know we're here." Jimmy's voice had dropped to a whisper.

"They know."

"How come you're so sure?"

"Because we know *they* are—dammit!"

"What is it, Slocum?"

Slocum stared toward the horsemen slowly nearing the hill. "The one out front's called Half Eye by the Apache. Scar by the white man. If they decide to come after us, we'll be going up against the best mounted infantry troops who ever cocked a carbine."

The chill along Jimmy's spine went colder despite the scorching sun overhead. His heart pounded rapidly against his ribs. He felt a sudden urge to relieve his bladder, though he had done so less than a half hour ago. He peered through the shimmering heat waves; a dust devil danced through the prickly pear and ocotillo in the shallow valley. He didn't see the Indians. They had dropped from view behind a low swell in a bend of the creek three hundred yards away. The shadow from the stunted mesquites had lengthened noticeably, and still the Indians didn't appear. Relief surged through Jimmy's cramping gut.

"Looks like they've turned off, Slocum."

Slocum thumbed the hammer of his Winchester to full cock. "Hate to spoil your hopes, Jimmy. Remember what I said. Don't waste any ammunition. Make sure you have a clear target before you touch off a round."

Jimmy's heart skidded into his belly. Even as Slocum spoke, Jimmy spotted a quick flash of movement behind a greasewood clump just over a hundred yards downslope. "Slocum, I sure wish just once you could be wrong," he said, his voice shaky.

The Apaches were coming.

The town called Shiloh wasn't quite what Meg had thought it would be.

When they topped the narrow north pass leading into the wide basin below, she'd expected to see a shack in the middle of nowhere. She had always thought that was the sort of place where outlaws forted up.

Shiloh was considerably bigger than that.

It sprawled over maybe half a mile along the banks of the stream—almost a river here—fed by springs and snowmelt higher up in the mountain range Brazos had told her was the Sierra Madres. There were no streets as such. The dozen or so larger buildings, most made of adobe, a few of native stone from the surrounding mountains, seemed scattered at random as if tossed out by a giant's hand and left where they fell.

A few smaller structures that looked to be little more than shacks huddled on the south side of town, beneath the shade of obviously old, tall trees near the banks of the stream.

The biggest and most unusual building stood in what would have been the center of an ordinary town. Meg could tell even from this distance it wasn't a single house, but more like a compound. Four long, low, one-story buildings connected by thick adobe or stone walls formed a square, with a single, smaller structure isolated in the center beside a stone well.

A few trees, obviously old, many of them bearing the scars of lightning strikes, shaded the quadrangle buildings here and there. But there were no trees, brush, or any other structures except scattered outbuildings for a hundred yards in any direction from the compound. Meg thought that strange until it dawned on her that the land had been deliberately cleared. A few men in each of the four wings could hold off any attack by even a big force. And they could easily ride down or shoot anyone trying to escape.

The compound was more like a fort than living quarters. Meg knew it had to be Shiloh's headquarters. And that made it her destination. She committed the layout to memory as best she could in the brief time they waited on the rise. Escape from that place seemed impossible, but if there was a way she intended to find it. She turned her attention to the overall view of the settlement from the pass.

Shiloh was the biggest town Meg had seen since that one trip to Omaha she remembered from many years ago. Omaha had frightened her. Shiloh scared the hell out of her.

Even from this distance, with the buildings shimmering in heat waves, Shiloh seemed to reach out and touch her. It was an ominous touch, a feeling of unease and fear equal to any she had felt since that terrible day up on the Republican when these men had ridden up to her home. She shuddered inwardly, and finally managed to put a name to the aura the town emitted like the unwashed odor of the men around her. The word was "evil."

Even the steep mountains surrounding the basin on all sides, and through which they had ridden the last few days, had left her uneasy. The mountains were rocky and craggy, but heavily timbered. Piles of downed trees and boulders bigger than horses cluttered the few passable trails. The mountains had seemed to close in on her, squeezing her breath away, during the ride through them on twisting switchback trails.

Meg was out of her element here. As a child of the plains, the endless sweep of rolling grassland and few trees, she had no knowledge of mountains. She sensed that even if she did somehow manage to escape Shiloh, survival afterward would be all but impossible. Alone in these peaks and unexpected canyons, she would soon become hopelessly lost. If Shiloh and his men didn't find her and she didn't starve to death, something in these mountains would kill her. The memory of the deep cough from the dense timber two days back still chilled her bones.

"Mountain lion," Shiloh had said. "There's a lot of them in these parts, some of them man-killers." It might have been a lie designed to frighten her. If it was, it had worked. The image of being torn to pieces by a big cat's jaws—possibly while still alive—lingered in the part of her brain that dwelt on horrors.

Her best hope for escape now sat in the saddle partway up the canyon wall, alone as usual. But Brazos had said he couldn't help her "now." She clung to the faint hope that soon "now" would come.

The approach along the trail below of the big, garrulous man with the bad foot and his skeletal one-armed companion interrupted her thoughts.

Hank reined in beside Shiloh, removed his hat, and wiped a bandanna across his face. "Damn sight cooler up here in the high country, Shiloh," he said. "Thirty degrees, most likely. Like ridin' out of the desert into a snowbank—"

"Stow the chatter, Hank," Shiloh interrupted. "Report."

"Dutch and his boys are back. They done near as well as we did, maybe better, the last few months. Manson and his bunch ain't here yet. No sign of Scar."

Shiloh shrugged thin shoulders. "Scar will be along in good time. He wants what we have to trade."

Meg saw the big man's gaze flick quickly to her, then away. His quick glance at the word "trade" added to the cold lump in her belly. Was she some part of a deal Shiloh had worked out with this Scar fellow, whoever he was?

"Dutch have any trouble?" Shiloh asked.

Hank shrugged massive shoulders. "Not much. Taylor and Johnson got dead. Jorge's got a hole in him, but not a bad one. Dutch said it was a fair enough trade. He got better'n half a hundred rifles and another wagon load of ammunition out of the deal."

Shiloh nodded, apparently satisfied. "He's right. Fair trade. All quiet down below?"

"Quiet as hungover church mice."

"Might as well get moving then." Meg started, heart pounding, as Shiloh drew the sharp, thin-bladed knife from his belt sheath and held it against her throat. She braced herself, wondering what the cut would feel like, how long it would take her to die—

The blade slipped between her neck and the rawhide reata still looped around her throat. The rawhide parted under a quick slice of the knife.

"There is no longer a need for this," Shiloh said as the severed reata dropped away. "There's no place you can run now, anyway." He paused for a moment, letting the razor's edge of the steel rest against Meg's throat. "And you don't want to try again. You wouldn't like how that would turn out."

Meg swallowed in relief as the blade dropped away. She raised her hand to massage the skin the reata had chafed and burned for so many days she'd lost count. Just not having the noose around her neck brought a surge of relief, a false sense of freedom.

"Let's move out, men," Shiloh called as he reined his horse toward the long, rocky grade of the descent into Shiloh.

A sudden chill gripped Meg even as they rode from the shade of the pines into the broiling heat of the basin floor. She stiffened in the saddle, her heart in her throat. She didn't know how she knew, but she knew.

Jimmy was in trouble. . . .

The Apaches were close now.

Jimmy's fingers felt cold against the receiver and trigger of the Winchester, and went colder at every flicker of movement amid the jumble of boulders and brush on the hillside below. Twice he had tried to line the sights of the rifle, but both times the target was gone in less than a heartbeat.

Jimmy strained his hearing, but no sound came from the slope except an occasional faint rustle of brush or dry grass.

These Indians weren't fighting the way they did in the books. No quick charge on horseback, whooping and yelling. Jimmy would have welcomed that. At least it would beat this waiting, not knowing—his breath caught in his throat.

Forty yards downslope, a man's moccasined foot showed clearly through a break in the limbs of a small juniper. The sights of the Winchester quavered as Jimmy drew a bead. He remembered Slocum's instructions, drew a deep breath, and let it out slowly. The sights stopped shaking. He stroked the trigger.

At the sharp crack of the .38-40, the moccasined foot bounced and a yelp of pain sounded. Jimmy worked the action, racked a fresh round in the chamber—and all hell broke loose.

Half a dozen Apaches rushed them, ducking and dodging, fanned out on the slope below. Jimmy fired at one man, rushed the shot, missed clean, and the Indian ducked behind a boulder. Slocum's rifle blasted once, twice, before Jimmy could work the action.

A slug from off to the right kicked a stone near Jimmy's head and whined off into the distance. He started, but forced himself to ignore the near-miss. The Apache he had fired at made a mistake; he showed his head and shoulders above the rock, the muzzle of his rifle swinging toward Jimmy.

This time, Jimmy didn't rush the shot. He heard the slap of lead against flesh, and saw the man wince and drop back behind the boulder. Jimmy had to duck himself as a volley of lead ripped into and over the rocks before him.

Slocum's Winchester cracked once more. Then a sudden silence fell over the hilltop. Jimmy's ears rang from the sharp crack of rifles from both defenders and attackers. Jimmy's heart hammered against his ribs; sweat trickled from beneath his hat into his right eye. He swiped a sleeve across his face, trying to clear the sting and blurred vision from his shooting eye.

Jimmy felt a blow against his lower leg, then heard the throaty roar of a big-bore rifle. The shot had come from his right, not from in front—he twisted and blinked through the watery blur toward the hillside across the stream. He saw an indistinct shape move and started to raise his rifle.

"I got him, Jimmy," Slocum said. A second later, the heavy boom of Slocum's big Peabody jarred the ground under Jimmy. The distant figure lifted from its feet and flung backward, arms and legs sprawling, then slid a few feet down the hill.

The silence that followed the echoes of the Peabody's blast was almost as deafening as the muzzle report of the rifle itself.

Jimmy thumbed cartridges into the .38-40's loading port; as he did so, he felt the first dull burn from the calf of his leg and realized he had been hit. He gritted his teeth and ignored the burn. His vision completely cleared, he flicked his gaze over the slope beneath. He saw no movement, no indication that any living thing was out there, let alone a bunch of men.

The shadows cast by the rocks and brush had lengthened by a handspan before Slocum finally spoke, his voice barely a whisper.

"You all right, Jimmy?"

Jimmy had to try twice to get the words past the cotton in his mouth. "Think—they got me—in the leg. Don't reckon it's bad."

"Keep a sharp eye downslope. I'm going to sidle over and take a quick look."

Jimmy felt the touch of steel and heard the slight rip as Slocum's knife cut through the cloth of his pants leg. Fingers gently probed the wound.

Slocum grunted in relief. "Like you said, not bad. Slug just clipped the muscles of your calf. A foot lower it could have cut your Achilles tendon and crippled you for life. You're bleeding some." Jimmy stared downslope, still halfway in disbelief that he'd actually been shot. He felt something snug up around his leg, and realized Slocum had tied a cloth over the wound.

"I don't see nothing, Slocum," Jimmy said. "Where are they at?" He didn't realize Slocum had moved back to his original position until the answer came from his left.

"I'd say they pulled back to parley, try to decide whether it's going to be worth what it would take them to get us. I think we put four of them down, either dead or wounded. Good shooting there, by the way."

"What do we do now, Slocum? When'll we know?"

"We wait. We'll know by sunup. If they don't come at us by then, we can be reasonably sure they're long gone. If they do come at us, we'll be dead—but so will a number of them, and they know it." Slocum's tone was soft and calm, the words seemingly disinterested.

Jimmy cut a quick glance at the tall, black-haired man. "Ain't you worried?"

"Worried as hell, partner. But it's up to them, not us. Better get a long drink from that canteen beside you. It could be a long wait. Get some rest, sleep if you can. I'll stand first watch. Leg hurt?"

"Some. I reckon I can tolerate it. Glad it wasn't a bad hit, though."

"There's no such thing as a good gunshot wound, Jimmy. I'll take a closer look at it a bit later. You start hurting too bad, I've got a bottle of laudanum in the pack here."

Jimmy shook his head. "Can't shoot with that. Took that stuff once when I busted a rib. Made me groggy for two days. I can handle it, Slocum."

"Yes, amigo, I suppose you can," Slocum said. The confidence in Slocum's tone made Jimmy feel better—almost good, for a kid who'd just shot two men and got shot himself. "Get some rest now. I'll let you know if anything happens and when it's your turn to stand watch."

"Ain't real sure I can sleep, Slocum. Kinda wound up and more'n a tad nervous. And that leg's stingin' a little."

Slocum smiled. "Know how you feel, partner. But at least get as comfortable as you can and give your eyes a rest. If anything moves out there, I'll wake you."

"Reckon that might help." Jimmy folded a blanket to use as a pillow, put his rifle close by his right hand, and closed his eyes.

Within minutes, Slocum heard the boy's steady, regular breathing. As his gaze swept the brushy, rugged slope and the countryside visible around the low hill, he half envied the youth. The ability to drop quickly into a sound, deep sleep was little more than a distant memory to Slocum.

But then, he reminded himself, no two men were alike— and Jimmy was well on his way to becoming a man. A strong one, wise beyond his years. The liking he'd had from the first time he'd seen him for the boy who had the courage and determination of a badger had grown to warm fondness. That bothered Slocum as much as it pleased him. Getting too close to someone was dangerous. It hurt too much if they got killed.

All was quiet downslope.

Jimmy came awake, instantly alert and reaching for his rifle, at the light touch on his shoulder.

"See 'em, Slocum?"

"Nothing moving out there but a prowling coyote. Your time to stand watch. I could use a bit of rest. Wake me if you see anything the least bit suspicious."

"Okay." Jimmy glanced at the stars and the half crescent of the moon low in the west. The sky told him it was nearly three in the morning. He was startled he had slept so long. The moonlight was faint and the shadows black where the moon didn't touch. His eyes weren't as good as Slocum's, but he didn't think anyone else's were either. He'd be able to see well enough, at least until the moon set. He shivered slightly, wondering again how this country could be hot enough to melt lead by day and cold enough to chill the blood at night. He draped the blanket he had used as a pillow across his shoulders and sat, rifle across his lap, staring into the patches of light and shadow before him.

It was going to be a long night.

The eastern sky had taken on a faint gray tinge when Jimmy's muscles twanged and his heart jumped.

In the near distance, maybe two hundred yards out, a dark spot—then another—appeared suddenly, in the exact spot he had been watching. A third joined, then a fourth, and he caught a glimpse of something white flash weakly in the starlight.

"Slocum, they're back. Down yonder. Couple hundred yards," Jimmy said softly, afraid his trail partner might not hear him.

He needn't have worried. Slocum was awake in an instant. The double click of his Winchester hammer drawn to full cock seemed loud in the still predawn air.

Slocum's gaze followed the point of Jimmy's rifle muzzle. After a couple of heartbeats, Slocum sighed and lowered the hammer. "Those aren't Apaches, Jimmy. What you see is a man's best friend in Indian country."

"What?"

"Pronghorn antelope, come in for water and graze. That means the Apaches are gone, or the pronghorns wouldn't be here. Apaches and antelope are long-standing enemies."

Jimmy's breath went out in a whoosh. He hadn't realized he had been holding it. "They could of took us, Slocum."

"They could have. And likely would have, after we put a few of them down. My guess is they knew it would cost them more casualties than they could afford. And that they had something more important to do."

In a few moments, the light had grown enough that Jimmy could make out the familiar shapes he had seen often in the rolling grasslands to the north. He lowered the muzzle of his rifle, relief flooding through his muscles.

"Sorry I woke you up, Slocum. I should have waited till I was sure."

"No, Jimmy, you did exactly the right thing. When in doubt, sing out." Slocum glanced toward the glow in the east. "How's the leg?"

Jimmy flexed his foot, tightened the muscles of his right calf. "Hurts some. Not bad."

"Can you ride?"

"Easier'n I can walk."

"Then let's water the horses, take a quick look at that wound of yours, and move out. I want to see which direction Scar and his bunch went."

By the time the sun cleared the horizon by a handspan, they were two miles from the rocky hill where they'd made their stand. Slocum rode silently, following the pony tracks they had found at daybreak. Specks of dark, almost black, red occasionally dotted the trail.

Slocum reined in and motioned Jimmy close. He pointed to one of the dark spots. "What's that tell you, Jimmy?"

The boy leaned from the saddle, squinted, then dismounted. He favored the right leg a bit as he knelt beside the trail, but Slocum was reasonably sure it wouldn't hamper Jimmy for long. It was a shallow wound, and if it didn't get infected it would heal quickly. At least it didn't seem to bother Jimmy that much on horseback.

After a moment, Jimmy stood. "One of 'em was still bleedin' when they come past here. Blood's near dry. So's the pony droppings. I make it six hours, give or take, since they rode past."

Slocum smiled at the youth. "Jimmy, I thought you had the makings of a first-rate tracker. Now I'll have to take that back. You're already past the 'makings' stage."

Jimmy's chest puffed a bit with pride, but the feeling soon drained away as he looked up at Slocum. The tall man's smile faded as quickly as it came; Slocum sat in the saddle, staring toward the southwest.

"Problem, Slocum?" Jimmy asked as he mounted.

"Could be. I've always leveled with you, Jimmy. I'm not going to change that now. Scar was on a raid when he stumbled on to us. When he finishes that raid, he'll be looking to trade. This man Shiloh trades with Scar, has for years. Which means we have to get your sister out of there before Scar rides in.'' Slocum turned in the saddle to face Jimmy. "One of the things Scar really likes to trade for is blond-haired women."

Jimmy's face paled.

"Sissy's a blonde," he said.

7

The evil feel of the town named Shiloh clamped harder in Meg's belly as the small procession made its way toward the big compound in the center of the settlement, a flag with crossed bars and stars on a field of red fluttering above the south, or front, wall.

A few brown-skinned people in ragged clothes, tattered blankets tossed across a shoulder and wearing big-brimmed, floppy hats, disappeared quickly and fearfully along the way as Shiloh and his men rode into view.

A few of the Mexicans, heavily armed and obviously part of Shiloh's gang—or perhaps some other outlaw bunch—lounged against buildings and raised hands in casual greeting as the slight horseman passed by.

Others, tough-looking white men with faces darkened from wind and sun, lifted fingers to hat brims in a sort of military salute to Shiloh. He returned the salutes, sometimes calling the men by name. For the most part, their gazes settled on Meg. She could feel the weight of raw lust in their stares as she rode past.

One bearded, broad-shouldered, and dirty tough strode up to Meg, put a hand on her thigh, and grinned. He was missing two front teeth; the remaining teeth were yellowish brown and chipped.

"Hey, Colonel," the man called, "looks like you brung us some mighty fine pussy this time—"

"Remove your hand, Marks!" Shiloh snapped. "This woman is not for the likes of you—or anybody. Touch her and I'll stake you to a wagon wheel and roast you alive, *sabe*?"

Marks's hand yanked away as if he had grabbed a hot stove. "Yes, sir, Colonel. You're the boss."

"Don't forget that, Marks. It will save you a lot of grief."

The man strode away, trying to look indifferent and tough, but Meg could tell he was badly shaken. What was it about this little man called Shiloh, she wondered, that put such fear in the hearts of bigger and stronger men? And what did Shiloh mean that nobody was to touch her? When had that order gone into effect? Not one man in the gang, not even Shiloh, had tried to force her legs apart in the last week. She welcomed the absence of humiliation and pain of the unwanted attention, but now wondered: If they didn't plan to use her, what did they have in mind?

She forced the questions away. For the moment, it was enough that they wouldn't be bothering her. She tried to concentrate on the details of the town itself; the overall layout remained fresh in her mind from her observations up on the pass.

All the buildings seemed to serve a function. They rode past a large livery stable, big enough to accommodate a bigger herd of horses than she'd seen in her entire life, complete with an expansive, well-equipped blacksmith shop attached. Also alongside the livery sprawled a wagon yard only half full despite the three large Conestoga freighters and half a dozen smaller flatbed wagons inside. Most of the wagons appeared empty, but a few of the smaller rigs had canvas stretched over goods of some sort. An adobe fence that looked to be three feet thick and nearly six feet tall contained both the wagon yard and livery corral. The fence was notched at regular intervals with firing ports.

It was obvious that water was near the surface of the basin. From atop the pass, the floor of the basin had appeared almost a mirage, a blanket of deep green in a land of tans and browns below the tree line. She heard the distant bellow of a bull from the sizeable herd that grazed on the south end of the basin, watched over by a couple of men. In the settlement itself, stone wells and watering troughs stood beside almost every building. The river they crossed seemed clear and fresh, and was knee-deep to the horses. The abundance of water left her feeling even dirtier than before.

Two sturdy rock structures, little taller than a man, stood apart from the other buildings. They had no windows, and each had a single, heavy door held shut by iron straps locked tight by a big padlock. Meg had heard her father speak of such buildings from his military duty. Magazines, he'd called them. Containers for powder, primers, lead, loaded ammunition. The two were identical to the small, windowless building she had noticed at the northern edge of the larger compound ahead.

Meg winced inwardly as they rode past the first of two similar adobe buildings on opposite sides of what seemed to be the most heavily traveled path that would have been a street in a more organized town. The doors were open to catch any wayward breeze. The scent of stale beer, man-sweat, tobacco, and fresh wood shavings marked them as saloons. They were crowded, even this early in the day. From the first came the sound of a piano, tinny and out of tune, the laughter of men, and the squeals of women.

The scene she saw through the door of the second such building threatened to raise bile to the back of her throat; on a long table, two men held down a nude woman while a third lay atop her, his pants pulled to his knees, his buttocks bouncing. The sight itself wasn't nearly as revolting as the crude laughter and raucous cheers from the other men inside.

Meg cut a quick glance over her shoulder at Brazos, trailing behind as usual, as his horse passed the open doorway and the revolting scene on the table. He quickly turned his head away. Even from a few yards ahead, Meg thought Brazos looked as though he was about to vomit. She was grateful for them both when the building was behind them.

Shiloh reined his horse to a stop and raised a hand in front of the only two-story building in the town. A wide veranda ran the length of the upper story. Two women stood there, both short and stocky, one with enormous breasts mostly revealed in a low-cut blouse. The other had her skirt hiked above an overly plump knee. Both were swarthy, dark-skinned, but not Mexican—more Indian, Meg thought—and less than attractive.

One of the women called a greeting to the captain in a tongue Meg hadn't heard before. He replied in English.

"Hello, Josepha. Bring Carla out here, please."

The woman turned inside and a moment later appeared, shoving a white woman in front of her. The woman was about her own age, Meg thought, but painfully thin, with vacant, expressionless eyes in a face almost devoid of color.

"Pull Carla's blouse up, Josepha," Shiloh said casually.

Meg's breath caught in her throat as the cloth lifted above the white woman's chest.

She had only one breast.

Where the left had been was an ugly mass of angry, ridged scar tissue. Meg inwardly recoiled at the sight—then remembered Shiloh carried a tobacco pouch that seemed soft and supple. As if made of human skin. Meg shivered despite the oppressive heat.

"Carla and one of her friends tried to run away," Shiloh said, a steady gaze on Meg's face. "Carla was the lucky one." After a moment, he waved the small column forward.

They rode past two buildings that seemed to be supply depots or trading posts of some sort, before Shiloh reined in at the front wall of the quadrangular compound. He stiffened in the saddle, snapped a crisp salute to the Confederate battle flag above, then dismounted and strode inside. The faces of the waiting men reflected anticipation and eagerness.

He returned in a matter of minutes, a heavy canvas bag in his hand. "All right, men, you've earned a bit of recreation," Shiloh said, reaching into the bag. "An advance on your share of the take, to accommodate your immediate needs." He walked among the still-mounted men, handing each a few gold coins. "We'll split the rest when I've had time to do a full accounting of our proceeds and a final division when the trading is done. It appears, gentlemen, that we have had a highly successful season."

"Much obliged, Shiloh," the hulking Hank said eagerly, stroking the gold coins for a moment before tucking them into a shirt pocket. The others muttered or nodded their thanks, except Brazos. He calmly sat on his horse, saying nothing, his face void of expression as he pocketed his pay.

"My compliments on your efficiency and enthusiasm on this campaign, gentlemen," Shiloh continued. "You know where all the amenities are, and you know the rules. Care for your animals first. No drunken brawls or shooting each other." He glanced at Meg. "And a reminder. There are plenty of women in Shiloh to see to your needs. This one is no longer available. She shall not be touched. A guard will be watching over her at all times." Then Shiloh delivered a crisp salute. "Company dismissed."

With a whoop, Hank spun his horse and spurred the animal into a lope toward the livery, Joaquin at his stirrup, the walking skeleton called Ace trailing behind at an easy walk.

Brazos hesitated for the slightest of moments before turning his horse away, his gaze on Meg. She thought she detected a hint of worry and a silent message of encouragement in his amber eyes. Then he reined about and followed the others, holding his mount to a slow walk.

Meg realized with a start that she hadn't seen the Comanche, Injun Tom, since before they had crossed the river. He had simply disappeared somewhere along the way.

A stooped, white-haired Mexican man limped from the shadows of the quadrangle, bowed slightly, and muttered something to Shiloh, then waited. Meg slid from her mount's back at Shiloh's wave and followed him inside as the old Mexican led their horses away.

As her eyes adjusted from the bright sunlight to the dusky near-gloom of the interior, Meg became aware of another presence. She turned her head. Standing almost within arm's length was the muscular body of a middle-aged woman, her long, graying hair braided somewhat like Injun Tom's. The set of her mouth and glitter of dark eyes hinted at an unspeakable cruelty in the woman. A sheath at her broad hips held a long, heavy-bladed knife.

Shiloh nodded toward Meg. "Donna, see to our guest, please. You know the routine. Get her settled in the mid-house, get her a bath, a good meal, and some clean clothes. If she tries to escape, you may have her." Shiloh cast a knowing stare at Meg. "If you get any wild ideas, remember Carla. That was just one minor example of Donna's work. She enjoys that sort of thing a great deal."

The woman named Donna wrapped a big, strong hand around Meg's elbow, and led her through a back door to the center of the compound.

Meg saw at a glance that the "mid-house," as Shiloh called it, was little more than a prison. The windows were open, but barred with heavy iron straps barely an arm's width apart; the only door was thick hardwood secured by an iron strap held in place by a padlock that must have weighed a pound.

Donna twisted a key in the padlock, lifted the iron bar, and all but shoved Meg inside. The bar clanged down behind her. Meg heard the padlock snap shut. The woman had not said a word.

Meg took a deep breath. At least, if this was a prison, it would be a reasonably comfortable one. The air inside the thick adobe walls was pleasantly cool. The one-room building had space enough for several people.

Beds rested against three walls, the covers neatly made, chamber pots beneath each. Pegs set into the adobe served as hangers for clothing, and a squat dresser with three drawers stood against a wall beside each bed.

The expansive room also contained chairs and footstools, a table, a couple of kerosene lamps, a tiled basin beneath a water pump, and a porcelain pitcher on the basin shelf. Along one wall was an iron cookstove with a few pieces of firewood in a rack alongside, but no cooking utensils except a galvanized tin tub that would hold maybe seven or eight gallons of water.

Best of all to Meg's eyes at the moment, a deep, porcelain bathing tub waited near the stove. Several washcloths, towels, and the greatest luxury of all—a bar of real soap—lay on a low table beside the tub. The prospect of a long, hot bath lifted her spirits.

The pump was similar to the one in their Nebraska home. A splash of water from the pitcher for priming and a few strokes of the handle brought a trickle, then a stream, of fresh, cool water. She saw nothing in the way of drinking utensils, so she cupped her hands beneath the flow and drank until the edge was off her thirst.

She found matches and kindling, and had a fire going in the stove when the metallic rasp of a key in the padlock sent a quick tingle up her spine.

The woman called Donna strode in, dumped a bundle on one of the beds, and with a quick glower at Meg, left. She padlocked the door behind her.

While her bathwater heated in the metal tub, Meg rummaged through the bundle. It contained two simple housedresses, a pair of soft leather slippers with thin soles, and a wide bone comb, but no camisole or undergarments. Meg held one of the dresses to her shoulders and realized it would fit, if a bit snugly in places.

The bathwater was steaming by the time she figured out the meaning of the hole in the bottom of the tub nearest the wall. A wooden plug on a low shelf fit the hole; when pulled out after her bath, the water would drain onto the ground outside.

Under other circumstances, it would have been a luxurious arrangement.

She filled the tub and went to close the curtains. There were none, just the heavy glass pane beyond the iron bars of the windows. She would have no privacy here, but at the moment she didn't care that much. She had had precious little on the trail.

Meg stripped, tossed the filthy clothing she had worn into a corner, and sighed as she lowered herself into the tub. The warm water caressed her skin. She closed her eyes and leaned back, savoring the moment, letting the heat soak the soreness from her muscles and loosen the outer layers of dirt.

After a time she opened her eyes, reached for a washrag and soap, and scrubbed until her skin turned a bright pink. The act of bathing made her aware of her own body; her breasts were firm, but not as large as her mother's had been, her waist narrow until it flared into trim but muscular hips.

Her legs somehow seemed longer than she remembered.

She scrubbed longer than usual at the triangle of dark-blond hair at her crotch, and then at her upper thighs, stopping only when it became painful. At least on the outside she felt cleaner, though she still imagined she could feel the wriggling of unseen things crawling up from there into her insides. She shuddered at the sensation, and tried to push it from her mind.

She lathered and scrubbed her hair and scalp. Realizing the water was beginning to chill, she reluctantly rinsed as best she could, then tugged at the wooden stopper until it popped free and the soapy water began to flow outside.

She stepped from the tub, reached for a towel—and realized she was being watched.

A broad, sunburned face at the window twisted in a leering grin. The man's tongue flicked across his lips. She didn't recognize him.

"Damn," she heard the man say, his voice thick, only slightly muffled by the glass windowpane, "the colonel finally put a mighty fine-lookin' *puta* in here. Sure wish I had that key. Come over here, honey. Show me that little blond snatch up close."

Meg ignored the leering face, toweled off, and slipped into one of the dresses. The material was light and airy and molded itself to her skin. The thin cotton strained against her breasts. As she had suspected, it was a bit small for her. But it was clean and new and smelled fresh. She ran the comb through her wet hair, tugging at a couple of particularly stubborn tangles, and looked around the room for a weapon.

She saw nothing that could be used except the pieces of firewood in the rack beside the stove. A sudden rush of exhaustion flowed through her muscles. She stretched out on the bed on her right side, her cheek resting against her arm, and immediately fell into a deep sleep.

Jimmy came awake at Slocum's light touch.

"Time to get moving, partner," Slocum said.

Jimmy sat up and stretched, rubbing his knuckles against sleep-scratchy eyes. The sun was still well below the eastern horizon. There was no hint even of false dawn. The only light, other than that from the stars overhead, came from the small fire Slocum had built.

It was the third morning since the brush with the Apaches, and still they seemed no closer to the distant purplish-blue Sierra Madres. Jimmy realized they had been traveling parallel to the mountain range instead of toward it. He asked Slocum why as the tall, lean man handed him a tin cup of coffee.

"Two reasons," Slocum said. "First of all, I don't know this country all that well. I have a general idea where Shiloh is, but not how to best approach it. Second, we need supplies. Once we're up in the Sierras, we don't know how long we'll be there."

Jimmy checked a quick flare of impatience. The only thing he wanted was to go get Meg, then kill a few men. But he was learning from Slocum, learning fast, and he had come to know and trust the man during the weeks they had ridden together. Slocum was no fool.

"Where we gonna get this stuff? Is there a town around somewhere?"

Slocum shook his head. "No town. But less than a day's ride south of here is the rancho of an acquaintance of mine. He knows this country better than anyone except maybe the Indians. We can resupply there and pick up another horse."

"Another horse? What do we need another horse for?"

A slight smile lifted Slocum's lips. "We have to have a good, fast mount for Meg, don't we?"

The single comment lifted Jimmy's spirits. Slocum was thinking way ahead. The need for another saddle mount hadn't crossed his mind. He told Slocum as much.

"It would have, Jimmy. It was just a matter of time until you had it all thought through."

That was another reason Jimmy found himself increasingly proud to ride with this man. Slocum never scolded, upbraided, or put a fellow down when he made a mistake or didn't think something out to the end. He could tease at times, but never with spite, just with the right touch of irony or humor. It was a mighty comfortable way to learn. Jimmy learned from him every day. It might be something as simple as reading sign, or the name of a strange plant, or how to patch a saddle, or as complicated as stripping and cleaning a rifle. When to talk and when to keep quiet.

Slocum was still a strange man, one who didn't fit any special mold, Jimmy thought. He could kill in the blink of an eye and without regret. Other men seemed to know instinctively that he was a dangerous man not to be messed with, a *pistolero* without fear no matter what the odds. Yet never careless. If he could ride around a fight, he'd ride. When he fought, it was with a plan, with no quarter given and none asked. He fought to kill.

Jimmy studied the face of his teacher and friend. Slocum was, Jimmy supposed, a good-looking man; he never failed to draw the attention of girls or women when one was around. But he didn't take advantage of his looks to go lifting a skirt every chance he had.

That was part of the streak in him Jimmy couldn't quite get a handle on. It wasn't a soft streak, by any means. More of a gentle, patient streak, whether he was teaching young horses or greenhorn kids. With other men, Jimmy would have been afraid to ask dumb questions. With Slocum, it was as if there was no such thing as a dumb question.

Jimmy was full of questions now, but he didn't try to ask them with his mouth full of breakfast. This was a big breakfast, which told Jimmy they had a long day ahead. Jimmy put away a second helping of bacon, fried potatoes—the last spuds from the grub sack—and Slocum's water biscuits, heavy, crusty, and filling as all get-out. Jimmy figured a man could live several days on just the biscuits alone.

Dawn was beginning to show when they finished cleaning up the campsite, stowed their gear on the packhorse, and swung into the saddle.

Several times as they rode, through the cool morning and blazing hot afternoon, Jimmy almost spoke. But each time he realized that Slocum was thinking on something, and thinking hard. Anything Jimmy had to say could wait.

The sun was three-quarters of the way down toward the hazy mountains when they topped a rise and saw the buildings clustered in the wide valley below. A *vaquero* suddenly appeared beside them, startling Jimmy, but Slocum merely nodded a greeting. The weathered *vaquero* reined his mustang into step with them.

The man waiting in the shadows of the veranda was almost as tall as Slocum, with a full head of snow-white hair riffling in the breeze and a curved pipe sticking out from under a handlebar mustache. A Smith & Wesson revolver nestled against his left hip, its holster and grips showing wear.

Up close, Jimmy could tell the man was old, yet he still carried himself erect, back straight and shoulders squared. The brown eyes in the weathered face held the confidence and knowledge of a man who had seen much in his lifetime. The eyes sparkled as a wide smile deepened the wrinkles in his face.

Slocum removed his hat, catching Jimmy by surprise. It was a gesture of respect Slocum had shown no man before now, and they had met more than a few on the long journey. Jimmy bared his own head, following Slocum's lead.

"*Buenos dias, Don Viejo,*" Slocum said.

"*Buenos dias, Slocum.* It has been a long time. Please, step down. *Mi casa es su casa, amigo.*"

Jimmy got another surprise when Slocum allowed the *vaquero* to take the reins of both horses and lead them away. Slocum always tended his own mounts and secured his own gear. Jimmy recognized the action as a sign of complete trust.

He followed Slocum up the two steps onto the veranda. Slocum and Don Viejo shook hands warmly. "It is good to see you again after so many years, Slocum. And your friend?"

"Don Viejo, James Daniel Forrest, of Nebraska Territory."

The rancher offered a hand. Jimmy took it, surprised at the strength in the old man's grip. "A pleasure to meet you, Señor Forrest. A man who rides with Slocum is welcome here. Please, come inside. Perhaps we can find something to cut the dust of the trail."

The interior of the sprawling adobe was cool, the air fresh, with a faint, pleasant hint of pipe tobacco. Don Viejo led them through a dining room larger than Jimmy's whole house had been, then down a long hall to a smaller room lined on two sides with books and soft, comfortable chairs. Whatever Don Viejo might be, Jimmy thought, he sure wasn't broke.

JAKE LOGAN

Don Viejo and Slocum chatted in Spanish for a moment. Jimmy couldn't follow the conversation, but realized the Don must have spoken to him. The old man's eyes were on his, the thick gray brows arched.

"Sorry, sir," Jimmy said apologetically. "I don't speak Spanish."

"My mistake, Señor Forrest. Forgive me. I merely asked if you wish something to drink? Perhaps join Slocum and me in a tequila?"

"No, sir, thank you. I—I don't drink liquor yet. Don't reckon I've earned the right, even if I liked the taste of it. Which I don't."

"Ah, then. You shall have Pensativa's specialty. Fresh water with lime juice and a twist of cinnamon. Quite refreshing, Señor Forrest."

"Sir? Would you mind calling me Jimmy? I'm sort of more used to that."

The aging rancher nodded pleasantly, then called a Señora Somebody, and added some soft Spanish words. A few minutes later, a tall, strikingly pretty woman strode into the room with glasses and a bottle on a silver tray. She placed the drinks on the table before the Don, then smiled at the three men. Her gaze seemed to linger on Slocum for a moment, and his on her. She left.

The Don handed Jimmy a tall, cold glass with a reddish twist of something in it, along with a quarter of a lime. He waited as Jimmy took a tentative sip; it was like nothing he had ever tasted, sweet but tart, light on the tongue.

"It's good, sir. Real good," was the best Jimmy could manage. He sipped at his lime water as the Don poured Slocum and himself a generous amount of tequila into two glasses. A slice of lime and a small salt dish sat beside the bottle.

Jimmy watched, fascinated, as the two men touched a finger to the salt, then to the tongue, downed the tequila, and followed it up with a bite into the flesh of the lime.

Slocum sighed in contentment. "Still nothing but the best for you, I see, Don Viejo."

"A man should enjoy his declining years, my friend." The two slipped back into Spanish. Jimmy guessed from the tone of the conversation they were exchanging news of each other's lives and maybe some idle chatter.

After a time, Slocum leaned forward and set down his glass.

"Don Viejo, I come to ask a favor," Slocum said in English.

"Name it and it is yours, if possible," the Don said. Jimmy sensed Slocum had steered the conversation back to English for his benefit. He made it a point to listen closely.

"We are looking for the hideout of the man who calls himself Shiloh," Slocum said. "He has Jimmy's sister. We intend to get her back from his stronghold. Do you know of it? And him?"

Don Viejo frowned. "That man is a plague of grasshoppers upon the land. *Bastardo.* He raids Mexicans and Anglos alike, trades the loot for guns and ammunition." He cut a quick, apprehensive glance at Jimmy. "And he trades women. With the outlaw Apache Scar, for the silver and gold Scar steals from the mines to the south. I am sorry to have to say those words, friend Jimmy."

Despite the sinking feeling in his gut, Jimmy nodded. "It's no big surprise. Slocum and me figured as much. I just was sort of hopin' we was wrong."

The rancher held Jimmy's gaze for several heartbeats, the brown eyes soft and sympathetic. "I shall place my *vaqueros* at your disposal, should you wish. I have perhaps fifty good, tough men who would gladly help stomp that bed of snakes. We can gather another fifty or so from ranchos bordering mine."

"Thank you, sir, but I reckon this is a job for just Slocum and me. Two men might have a chance to get her out. If a whole bunch come at them, they might kill her." He lowered his gaze. "I ain't ready to face that just yet."

"There is more you must hear," Don Viejo said. "I'm afraid I have news that is not good. Within a week, Scar will have finished his raids on Mexican mines and be on his way to Shiloh to trade—"

"But sir," Jimmy interrupted, "how could that be? Slocum and me, we tangled with Scar's bunch not four days ago."

Don Viejo turned a questioning gaze toward Slocum, who quickly filled him in on the details of the fight at the hill. As Slocum finished, Don Viejo nodded.

"I do not doubt for a moment that you fought Scar, my friends. But not his main force. Scar has many more than twenty warriors at his disposal. Perhaps a hundred, perhaps more, under the command of Scar's half-brother, Hoh-Shay. The larger force passed within two days' ride of here a month ago. The group you fought was more than likely a scouting party, making sure there would be no organized force to threaten Hoh-Shay's return."

Don Viejo leaned back, scratched a match, and lit his pipe. "The mine raiders will be at Shiloh within the week. If you are unable to rescue your sister by then, I fear you will never see her again."

"That's why we came to you, Don Viejo," Slocum said. "I know nothing about Shiloh's stronghold. If there is anything at all you can tell me about it, I would be in your debt."

"There are no debts between us, my friend." The rancher puffed at his pipe for a moment, then said, "Are you aware of the grand plans of this man called Shiloh?"

"Beyond personal enrichment from raiding, no," Slocum said.

"Then you must hear me out, for many innocent lives are at stake. He has formed an alliance not only with the renegade Apaches, but also with some Mexican Indian tribes—and embarrassingly, with the *commandante* of the *federales* in this district. When their combined forces are strong enough, and well enough equipped, including artillery pieces, they will attack the Anglos on three fronts. Scar will arm the Indians, including those on the reservation, to sweep through Arizona. Shiloh's men will strike north through New Mexico, cutting rail lines and trade routes to California and its gold fields and supply ports. The *federales* under our renegade *commandante* will invade Texas and Arizona with the intent of restoring them to Mexico.

"In short, my friends, within two years, possibly less—if he is not stopped—the Southwest will be the new Confederate States of America. With the man named Shiloh as supreme dictator."

Jimmy heard Slocum's quick intake of breath. He was still trying to make sense of what Don Viejo had said, and not getting anywhere. "But Don Viejo," Jimmy said, "won't the American army put a quick stop to that?"

"A stop, yes. But not a quick one. Much blood will be shed, most of it from innocent civilians. And it could trigger another all-out war between the United States and Mexico."

Slocum downed another quick shot of tequila, this time without benefit of salt or lime. His brow furrowed. "That throws a whole new light on things, Don Viejo," he said.

"Sir," Jimmy said, "I don't want to sound like a—well, like a smart-alecky kid. But how do you know this?"

"A legitimate question, Jimmy. I do not, of course, have all the details. But I do have a considerable network of spies, informants, on both sides of the border."

"Then why not tell the American army? Or the leaders of your own country?"

Don Viejo frowned. "More than a month ago, I dispatched my two most trusted men—my two sons—to inform the authorities. One went to Arizona, the other to El Presidente in Mexico City. Will they believe? I do not know. The scheme is so preposterous that I would not believe it myself, if I did not know it to be true."

"The Don has a point, Jimmy," Slocum said. "The whole idea is just too big, too absurd, for anyone in authority to grasp. Only a madman, and a shrewd one at that, could come up with such a plan. The problem is, it might work. At least for a time."

"Make no mistake, Slocum," Don Viejo said, "this man who calls himself Shiloh *is* a madman. He actually believes he can do it. And that makes him more dangerous than any schemer of sound mind." The Don sighed. "But first things first. In this case, Jimmy, your sister. The rest we shall worry about later."

He stood, strode to a rolltop desk in the corner, and retrieved a cylindrical parchment from a cubbyhole. He moved the silver tray to one side of the table and spread the map. "For the young lady's sake, we have no time to waste, my friends. I will share with you what I know. Let us begin. . . ."

8

"Slocum," Jimmy said solemnly as the buildings of Don Viejo's ranch grew small in the distance behind them, "this thing has all of a sudden got bigger than just you, me, and Sissy, ain't it?"

Slocum's brow furrowed. "Yes, it has."

"Can he do it? This Shiloh feller, I mean? Make a war and a new country and all?"

"Not a new country. Things have changed since the Confederacy tried and failed to do the same thing—cut the West in half. But there's a real chance he could make a war between Mexico and the United States. Relations between the two countries have been strained for years."

"I don't know nothin' about politics, Slocum, and don't care to know much. But I reckon the Don's right. Whether he does or don't, a lot of people are gonna get killed along the way."

"Yes, they will. Which makes it all the more important that we put Shiloh down. Cut off the head and the rest of the snake dies. So for us, it doesn't change a thing. We still do what we set out to do." Slocum glanced at Jimmy. The boy rode with his back straight, his gaze sweeping the countryside, but there seemed to be a bit of a slump to his shoulders.

For a time, neither spoke, each wrapped in his own thoughts. The packhorse, laden with fresh supplies, and the

sleek sorrel race mare bearing a lightweight Mexican saddle
trailed behind. Don Viejo would accept no money for the supplies or the race mare. The mare, he had said, was a loan, to
be returned when possible. Realistically, Slocum thought, the
Don should have said "if possible." But if somehow they did
manage to get Jimmy's sister out, she would be better mounted
than anyone in Mexico. Or the States, for that matter.

Jimmy caught Slocum's gaze with a surprisingly calm, level
stare. "Can we get her out? Way the Don talked, ain't nobody
gonna get into that place and out again alive."

"Nothing's ever impossible, Jimmy. I've not lied to you,
and I'm not going to start now. The odds are against us, but
there's always a way. We just have to find it. The first thing
we have to do is get your sister out and safe. Then we'll worry
about the rest of it. Including Shiloh."

Pain flared in Jimmy's eyes, but the set of his jaw never
wavered. "Slocum, do me a favor? If we"—his voice caught
a bit—"can't get her out, shoot her for me. She's suffered
enough. We can't let that Apache have her, not from what the
Don says about how he treats white women." His voice had
gone so soft, Slocum had to strain to hear him. "I think she'd
want it that way. I can't kill my own sister, Slocum. I just
can't."

Slocum nodded solemnly. "If worse comes to worst,
Jimmy, I'll do it. But only as a last resort. Now, we won't
discuss it again. A man who rides into a tough spot thinking
he's going to lose is doomed to fail. So we concentrate instead
on how we're going to succeed."

Jimmy rode for a moment in silence, then said, "If worse
comes to worst like you say, and you have to make a choice,
kill Shiloh instead. I reckon Sissy'd understand that a whole
bunch of lives is worth more than one."

A tightness closed around Slocum's chest. Once again he'd
underestimated Jimmy. The boy had made a choice. To sac-
rifice the one person nearest his heart, if necessary, to save the
lives of countless strangers. By God, Slocum thought, I'm riding with a man for sure now.

Slocum forced the words past the lump in his throat. "It
won't come down to that, Jimmy. Because we won't let it."

He nodded toward the mountain range taking shape ahead.
"We'll camp in the foothills tonight and scout the place out
tomorrow. See if the Don's information is sound. Then we'll
put our heads together and come up with a plan of attack."

Jimmy fell silent for several more minutes, then said, "Slocum, no matter how this comes out, I ain't never met a better
man than you. Just wanted to get that said up front, case I
don't get to say it later."

Slocum's reply was a brief nod. He didn't trust himself to
speak. The knot in his throat had tightened up again.

Over the last three days, Meg had fallen into something of a
routine.

Twice a day, just before dawn and again in early evening,
the big woman Shiloh had called Donna brought food, lots of
it, and no two meals were the same. Mealtimes had become
the most unsettling part of the day, at least while Donna was
in the room.

Donna never spoke; Meg wasn't sure the woman could. But
she would bring the food tray, put it on the table, and stand
for a moment staring at Meg's breasts, her thick fingers unconsciously toying with the knife at her belt. Donna's
breathing seemed to quicken at those times. Meg knew what
was going through Donna's mind. The idea of taking that knife
and slicing away one or both of Meg's breasts. She would
probably do it slowly. . . .

Meg's nerves still jangled for a bit after Donna finally left,
locking the door behind her. The first day, she had been so
shaken she couldn't eat until her food had grown cold. Since
then, it had become less of a struggle to push away the horror
and fear that came through the door with the big, broad-faced
woman.

In the late afternoon she bathed, ignoring the leers of the
guards through the curtainless windows. It was no longer embarrassing. Her sense of modesty had been beaten from her
on the trail. She simply ignored the looks and lewd comments.

After the morning meal, Donna gathered up the dress Meg
had worn the previous day and took it away for laundering;

in the evenings, she brought it back, along with freshly laundered—even ironed—cotton sheets.

Between breakfast and bath, Meg's biggest enemy was
boredom. There was little to do to keep her mind or her muscles occupied. She had fallen into the habit of pacing from
one side of the room to the other, then back, to relieve the
heavy feeling idleness brought to her legs.

Each evening she sat by the window in the growing darkness after sunset, letting the cool breeze from the mountains
above fan her skin. Then to bed, sometimes for a dreamless,
restful sleep, sometimes to the recurring nightmare that made
her live through the attack on the farm again. She woke from
those nightmares drenched in sweat, her jaws aching, hair plastered to her cheeks and neck.

The nightmares were less frequent now. Meg knew she
would never be completely free of them.

When she couldn't sleep, she worked on the only weapon
she had been able to improvise. It wasn't much—a sliver of
firewood smaller than her wrist and just over a foot long. She
had no tools, but soon discovered the rough spot on a leg of
the iron cookstove that would serve as a sort of rasp.

Another day or two, she figured, the makeshift wooden dagger would be ready. Already it had taken on the shape she
wanted, much like a tent peg, but smoother and with a sharper
point. Her only fear was that Donna might discover the stake.
She didn't know what the big woman's reaction would be if
she found it before Meg had a chance to plunge it into Donna's
heart. She didn't want to know.

A familiar voice from outside drifted through the window
as Meg settled into the tub for her bath on the afternoon of
her fourth day in the mid-house.

"I'll stand guard duty now, Bull." Brazos's voice was soft
but distinct on the slight breeze through the window. Meg
glanced up and saw the disappointment on the stubbled, leering face watching her.

"Boss ain't gonna like that, Brazos," Bull said. "Ever'
man's supposed to finish out his shift."

"I'll square it with the colonel should he ask," Brazos said
calmly. "You go on. There's a fandango cranking up down

at Maude's place. Lots of whiskey. And women who aren't behind lock and key.''

Bull didn't take much convincing after that. Brazos was alone on watch outside her window. Meg noticed that he kept his head turned away, not panting against the window like the others. She finished her bath more quickly than normal, toweled off, dressed hurriedly, and strode to the window.

''Brazos? Is that you?'' she asked in little more than a whisper.

''Yes, miss. I—I wanted to find out if you're all right. If you need anything.''

''That's kind of you, Brazos. Thank you, but I'm fine.'' She waited for a moment, but the young man didn't speak. ''Brazos,'' she finally said, ''do you have a real name?''

''You wouldn't believe me.''

''I might.''

''It's Bill. Bill Smith. I quit using it a long time ago because nobody believed it, thought it was an alias or something. But that's my given name.''

Meg caught a faint whiff of bay rum and soap through the open window. The young man had gone to the trouble of bathing and shaving before he came to her. For some reason, the idea touched her. ''May I call you Bill?''

''I'd like that, miss. It may take a spell for me to get used to answering to it, I haven't heard it in so long.''

''Please. Call me Meg. My real name is Mary Margaret, but my friends call me Meg.''

''All right—Meg.''

He still hadn't looked directly at her. His face was in quarter profile, looking off toward his left as he stood at the right side of the window. In fact, she recalled, he seldom looked directly at her.

''Bill, may I ask you something? You don't have to answer if you don't want to.'' She saw the almost impercepitble nod of his head. ''When—well, up in Nebraska. I know you didn't—didn't participate—when the rest of the men—took Mother and me. Physically, I mean. But I also seem to recall you never even looked, didn't watch. I've been wondering why.''

After several heartbeats, she decided he wasn't going to answer, and prepared to change the subject. He surprised her.

"It's hard to explain, miss—Meg. I don't know that I can." His voice had tightened in inner pain and turmoil. "It's just that—"

"Go ahead, Bill. I'm listening. And no one else will ever know, I promise."

He sighed, then seemed to gather himself. "It's just that since what happened to my little sister, what I saw through the window that day—whenever I see a man and woman"— he paused for a moment, as if searching for the strength to say it—"doing that, I don't see them. I see Allie. It's the same when I see a woman with no clothes on." Something seemed to glitter on his cheek; Meg realized with a bit of a start it was a tear. "I don't see a woman. I see Allie."

The tightness of his words, the obvious effort it took to get them out, touched Meg. "I think I understand, Bill," she said. "A thing like that must have been truly horrible to see."

"I've tried," he said after a moment. "There was a woman in Dodge City. A prostitute. I thought—well, it didn't work. When I tried she—she turned into Allie. I just couldn't do it. I'm not much of a man, Meg. I've come to accept that."

Meg's throat had tightened for some reason she couldn't explain. "I think we may have something in common, Bill. After what's happened to me, I don't think I ever want a man, at least that way, the rest of my life. Or at best, for a long time."

"I'm sorry I couldn't stop it—"

"You've already apologized for that once, Bill," Meg interrupted. "There was nothing you could do." She paused for a moment, then said, "I told you before you aren't like the others. You're not a killer, Bill Smith, or even, I think, a bad man at heart. Why don't you just leave this band of outlaws? Just get on your horse and ride away?"

Silence fell for a moment. When he spoke, his tone held a mixture of hopelessness and frustration. "I can't. I didn't find out until too late—when I'd already ridden with them too long—that nobody quits Dirk Dunnigan's bunch. Two men tried. About a month after I'd joined up. Dunnigan flew into a rage, called them deserters. The Comanche tracked them down, brought them back. Dunnigan had them stripped. He tied them to a wagon wheel, heads down over a small fire. They burned to death. It took a long time.''

The account sent a quick shiver up Meg's spine. She forced the mental image aside. "But maybe it's not too late. Maybe you'll find a chance.''

"Not as long as Injun Tom's around,'' he said in resignation. "Him and that spooky albino medicine horse he rides never quit a trail, Meg. I can't take the chance. Please forgive me. I'm just not—I'm a coward. There's no other word for it.''

"No, Bill. I don't think you're a coward. I think you've just been caught up in something that's too big for you to handle by yourself. Incidentally, I haven't seen that scary Indian since we started down the pass. Where is he?''

"Out riding the rim, I expect. He doesn't care much for the company of white men, and hates Mexicans even worse. He's a loner. Still fancies himself a big warrior. I've got to go now, Meg. The new guard's coming on duty.''

"Bill,'' she whispered urgently, "you asked earlier if there was something I needed. There is.''

"I can't give you a weapon,'' he whispered back. "It'd get us both killed. In a hard way.''

"Not a weapon. A book or two. If I'm going to be kept in this infernal jail, I *must* have something to occupy my mind or I'll go stark, raving mad.''

She saw his nod in the fading light. "I'll see what I can do. It will be tomorrow at best.'' He disappeared from view at the window. Another man, stubbled and missing a front tooth, took his place. Meg turned away from the window, ignoring the guard's remarks about her tits and ass.

When the sun set, she went to her bed in the darkness, unwilling to light a lamp, and lay there still hearing Bill Smith's voice in her mind, seeing the rather handsome shape of his face against the sunset.

Meg realized with a start that she had stopped thinking of how she might simply use the man called Brazos to help her escape. She had begun to think of him in different terms. As more than just another outlaw. It was an unsettling thought.

Jimmy stretched out alongside Slocum on the craggy, timbered crest of the Sierra Madre's east range and tried to gasp air back into his lungs. His leg muscles quivered from the steep switchback climb up the near-vertical mountainside. A warm trickle on his ankle told him the bullet gouge in his calf had opened again. It stung like the blazes from sweat-salt, but nothing he couldn't handle.

He noticed with some reassurance that Slocum was breathing harder than usual too. But the lean man had carried a double load up the slope—a spare water canteen, a grub pack, and the heavy Peabody rifle. Jimmy decided he still had a ways to go before he got to be as tough as Slocum, but he was gaining some.

As his breathing gradually slowed, Jimmy studied the wide basin below. He could believe what Don Viejo had said about the place having been a campsite for centuries. The grass was deep and green, and sunlight danced on the river and numerous streams that fed into it from the mountains around. The largest herd of cattle Jimmy had ever seen grazed in the far south end of the basin, two riders keeping watch. A remuda of a more than a hundred horses grazed between the cattle and the scattered buildings, also under the watchful eye of two mounted men.

Jimmy shifted his attention to the layout of the buildings. Again, Don Viejo had been accurate with his map and knowledge of the area.

The buildings weren't at all haphazardly scattered, except for the small shacks called *jacales* where laborers, farmers, and workers lived. The sturdier buildings were placed with military precision, each providing covering fire for the others.

No wonder the man called Shiloh had picked this spot for his stronghold. Only batteries of cannon spotted around the rims could inflict damage on the heavy buildings below, and even then, possibly not much. Jimmy didn't see how heavy cannon could be hauled over the mountains.

He twisted the top from a canteen and took a quick drink. The sun was almost directly overhead, and even in the shade of the pines and junipers, the still air was warm and dry. Climbing was thirsty work.

Slocum hadn't said a word since they'd hobbled the horses and made the long struggle up the mountainside. He lay now with the Peabody at his side, a brass spyglass on loan from Don Viejo in his hand, slowly sweeping the settlement below.

The glass stopped moving. Jimmy followed the direction it pointed, toward a series of buildings connected in a square at the center of town. A Confederate battle flag above the front of the square fluttered in the light breeze. A smaller building stood directly in the center of the square.

Slocum handed Jimmy the glass. "If Shiloh follows his usual pattern according to Don Viejo, that's where Meg will be, Jimmy. In the little house in the middle of the quadrangle."

Jimmy's fingers trembled as he took the glass. He had to fiddle with it for a moment before the scene below snapped into focus. Jimmy almost gasped aloud. He had never looked through a spyglass before; it was if he could almost reach out and touch the building. The glass put something right up in a man's lap.

His wonder over the glass quickly faded. His heartbeat increased. He was closer to Meg than he had been since that day up on the Republican, but he couldn't see a sign of her, even with the help of the glass. The windows of the building were dark from the overhanging roof.

"I don't see her, Slocum," Jimmy said.

"She has to be in that building. Or someone else is. Look closer. At the door. What do you see?"

Jimmy blinked, then put his eye back to the glass. "A big lock, looks like. Some kind of bar across the door."

"A place like where a person would keep prisoners," Slocum said.

Jimmy's spirits sank as quickly as they had risen. He handed the glass back to Slocum. "If she's in there, she might as well be on the moon. Dammit, Slocum, there's no way we can get inside that place.'' He pounded a fist in frustration on a gritty stone hard enough to bring pain.

"It looks that way," Slocum said, his tone flat. "But remember what I told you a while back. Nothing's impossible if we study on it long enough—" Slocum abruptly raised the glass, peered through it, and mouthed a curse. Jimmy squinted into the distance. A small figure, barely a dot to unaided eyes, stood on the south side of the big house.

"Shiloh Dunnigan," Slocum muttered through clenched teeth.

"Shoot the bastard, Slocum," Jimmy all but snapped.

"Not yet. Maybe I could reach him with the Peabody, but it's a good fourteen hundred yards. Even if I nailed him, that wouldn't help Meg. Getting her out is our primary objective." Slocum swung the glass toward the north, then to the south, finally back to the north.

It seemed to Jimmy that Slocum spent an hour just looking the place over. He forced his nagging impatience aside. Riding with Slocum was teaching him a lot of things. Patience was at the top of the list. An impatient hunter usually went home with no meat, Slocum said.

Slocum closed the glass and stowed it back in its round rawhide case. "Let's go, partner," he said.

"Where?"

"Back down the mountain. So we can circle way around and climb another one. Your leg's bleeding."

"Aw, it ain't nothin'."

"The hell it isn't. Hike your pants leg. I'll tighten that bandage some and patch it better when we get back down the hill."

Jimmy's jaw set in the first real show of defiance he had shown. "I tell you, Slocum, it ain't that big a deal. Now I don't want to argue with you, but we ain't got much time. It don't hurt that much."

Slocum leveled a steady, calm gaze on Jimmy. "I know it's not bleeding much. But think on it a minute. You're a good tracker. What's one way to track an animal—or a man?"

For a moment, Jimmy didn't answer, his brow furrowed. Then his forehead smoothed. "Blood trail."

"Right. Suppose one of Shiloh's sentries or scouts came across a few drops where there aren't supposed to be any. Would you rather be the tracker or the tracked?"

Jimmy pulled up his pants leg. "I reckon I see your point. Tighten her up."

Riding with Slocum, Jimmy had developed a taste for coffee. He hadn't had any in nearly two days, living on water and jerked beef and little else during the dry camps with no fire and the long scout along the rim of the basin. Right now, he thought as his belly rumbled, he'd nearly shoot somebody for a cup and a slab of fried beef—

A rattle of rifle fire from the basin floor snapped Jimmy's head around. From his station behind a fall of dead pines, he had been watching the moves of the horse and cow herd to the south. The shots yanked his attention back to the north end of the basin, nerves twanging. A dozen or so men stood or knelt a hundred yards from the northernmost building, firing rifles at the stumps of felled trees. Jimmy relaxed. It was only Dunnigan putting some of his men through target practice.

As he started to turn his head away, he caught a flicker of movement in the corner of his field of vision. The movement came from behind Slocum, a hundred feet from where the tall man knelt on one knee beside the narrow north pass trail, his spyglass trained on the outlaw stronghold below.

Jimmy squinted through the early morning light that dappled the pines and junipers, his heart thumping. After five minutes he decided his eyes were just playing tricks on him. He silently scolded himself for jumping at shadows, and had started to turn away when he saw it again—a flicker of brown through the brush, a speck of light on metal.

An instant later, Jimmy's heart leapt into his throat.

Just over a hundred yards away, the splotches of movement took form. A man clad in buckskins, sneaking up behind Slocum, a revolver in one hand and a big skinning knife in the other.

Jimmy choked back the yell of warning. He couldn't call out loud enough to be heard over that distance with the wind against him. He had to risk a shot; the man was within a few yards of Slocum, closing in on the stalk.

Jimmy thumbed the hammer of his .38-40 to full cock and waited for a clear shot. He knew it had to be a good one. The .38 slug wouldn't have much stopping power at that distance. Over the buckhorn rear sight of the Winchester, he saw the man crouch, ready to spring on Slocum from the rear. Another ragged volley of rifle shots sounded from the valley floor. Jimmy squeezed the trigger.

Through the powder smoke, he saw the man straighten from his crouch and look down at his side in surprise. At the same time, the slap of lead against flesh reached Jimmy's ears. The report of the .38-40 mingled with echoes of the gunfire from the basin. Before Jimmy could lever another round into the Winchester, Slocum leapt to his feet, turning, his right hand whipping from his belt and forward. Sunlight flashed on steel. The man in buckskins staggered a half step, looked down at his chest, then sank to his knees.

Slocum was on the big man before he finished falling. Jimmy saw Slocum grab at the man's chest as he yanked his head back; then steel flashed again.

Jimmy crabbed back from his perch. Taking care to keep the rim of the basin above his head, he ran, crouching, dodging boulders and downed trees. He was out of breath by the time he reached the side of the trail.

Slocum casually wiped the blade of his skinning knife on the man's shirt, and stood as Jimmy called out softly and stepped into the open, rifle at the ready.

The man on the ground was obviously Indian. He twitched feebly as bright blood gushed from his slashed throat, trickled from the puncture in his chest, and seeped into the buckskins below his left ribs where Jimmy's slug had hit. The man's eyes were still open, and bright with hate.

Jimmy's stomach churned. He'd never known there was that much blood in a man before.

"Good job, Jimmy," Slocum said. "He would have had me dead to rights. Guess I forgot Slocum's first law of survival: Watch your back. How did you manage to time that shot so the sound of the volley would cover it?"

Jimmy's voice was shaky. "Just blind luck. Had to take the shot then, or he'd have been on you."

A thin smile creased Slocum's lips. "Sometime the spirits smile on a man, Jimmy. They didn't smile on this Indian today."

The Comanche finally died, his last breath a hoarse gurgle. Jimmy hadn't realized it took a man so long to die with his throat cut.

"He was one of 'em," Jimmy said, studying the dead man's moccasins. "Recognize that track anywhere." The realization made it a lot easier, even satisfying, to accept the Indian's death. The bastard had it coming. One down, five to go, Jimmy thought.

Slocum sighed. "Let's get the body hidden and cover the blood. We don't want anybody stumbling over the corpse and wondering who killed him. Then we'll fall back away from this basin rim and work up a plan. We know all we need to know."

Jimmy leaned back against the trunk of a pine tree at the base of the tallest peak in the foothills and tried to still his swirling thoughts.

He should be tired, he knew, with all the climbing and the excitement of the Indian's death, but he felt fresh and alert. His leg had stopped bleeding sometime before yesterday. It didn't hurt anymore. Just felt a little tight in the calf muscle at times. Slocum said there was no sign of infection.

At least they'd pulled back far enough for a small, smokeless fire, a pot of coffee, and a bait of grub besides hard biscuits and harder jerky. He'd learned to take Slocum's advice and eat as much as he could, when he could.

An owl's distant hoot cut the early night, bringing a reply from closer by. A light, cool breeze ruffled the needles of the pine above his head. He'd finished cleaning his rifle and tending the horses while Slocum climbed the hill to take a look around.

The sound of gravel sliding beneath boots brought Jimmy's senses to full alert. He had the rifle in hand when Slocum strode back into camp, barely visible in the rapidly fading light. They had put the campfire out well before sunset.

Slocum squatted beside Jimmy, his frown visible even in the faint light.

"Trouble, Slocum?"

"Sooner than I'd hoped." Slocum pulled a cheroot from his pocket and lit the smoke, hands cupped around the match. Jimmy knew it was his last one. "Fires to the foothills to the south, Jimmy. Six of them."

"Scar's bunch?"

"Has to be. Dammit, they've gotten here sooner than I'd counted on. They'll be in Shiloh by sundown tomorrow."

Jimmy's heart sank. He knew only too well what that meant. More men, more guns—and less time left to Meg.

"How many?"

"Six fires would make it sixty or seventy men, Jimmy. That would mean Shiloh'll have at least two hundred men down there, with more on the way." He dragged at the smoke; Jimmy noticed Slocum kept the lit end cupped in his hand, so it couldn't be seen from any distance. "The Don was right. Shiloh never has fewer than a hundred men in his stronghold, not counting the Mexican peasants who do the dirty work for him."

Jimmy tried to study Slocum's face, figure out what the man was thinking. It was too dark now to read his features. "So what do we do?"

Slocum sighed. "We have no choice. Our hands have been forced, Jimmy."

Alarm flared in Jimmy's gut. "You ain't plannin' to ride out on Meg, are you?"

"If I were, would you go with me?"

"Hell, no." Jimmy's tone was sharp. "Not until Sissy's out of there alive. Or still there, dead. I'm goin' after her. Your help or not."

Slocum's soft chuckle surprised Jimmy. "That's what I figured you'd say, partner. I admire a man who never quits a trail or a job that has to be done." Slocum dragged at the cigarillo. "That job has to be done tonight, Jimmy. We're running out of time. . . ."

9

Jimmy scrunched down in the deep black shadows of the stable inside the compound and consciously tried to slow down the quick thump of his heart. It didn't work.

And if what he was about to try in a couple of hours didn't work, it wouldn't matter. He'd be dead anyway. Meg too, probably. He glanced again at the stars overhead. They hadn't moved much since the last time he'd checked.

Slocum hadn't much liked the idea of Jimmy coming down here alone. But there was no other way it could work. Slocum could no more look like a Mexican *peon* than he could look like a cow. He was too tall, too thick in the shoulders.

So it had been Jimmy who'd wrapped a torn blanket around his shoulders, serape-style, and started the long, nerve-wracking, muscle-wrenching stalk down the mountainside game trail into the basin. With his shorter build and in the near-blackness of the moonless night, and leaning back against a wall in the shadows, he could be mistaken for a Mexican peasant. Even though he had nothing that passed for one of the wide-brimmed sombreros they favored, it didn't matter that much. Not all of the laborers wore the big straw hats. Jimmy's own hat, battered by infrequent rainstorms, sun, and wind until the brim lost its stiffness and drooped all around, wouldn't seem that much out of place.

In their minds, the plan might work.

It had to. It was the only one they could come up with that stood a chance.

They knew that there was only one prisoner in the locked and barred house. The big woman who came before dawn carried only one meal tray. And when she delivered the late afternoon meal, she carried a bundle of women's clothes with her. Or so it looked through Don Viejo's brass spyglass.

Jimmy wasn't positive—yet—that Meg was the prisoner in the small house. Even through the powerful spyglass, neither he nor Slocum had been able to get a look at the woman inside. While it could be someone else, it made sense that it would be Meg. She was the most valuable living trade commodity Shiloh had, because the Apache named Scar paid handsomely for yellow-haired women. Don Viejo had said so. So had Slocum. That made it the gospel truth in Jimmy's mind. And fueled his determination to get her out.

Part of the reason for the rapid thump of his heart was the exertion of the long climb down, then forcing himself to shuffle along slowly across the open ground to the rear of the stables when every muscle in his body screamed at him to run. Part of it was pure, raw fear. But mostly, it was because he was now within just a few quick steps of Meg.

Slocum hadn't had to tell Jimmy twice that timing was the whole key to the operation.

The house-jail was unlocked only twice a day, by the stout woman bringing food. And the predawn meal was the only time the settlement wasn't crawling with people. It had to be early morning or never.

He had their escape route committed to memory. It was the same route he had followed into the basin, a twisting one-time game trail or possibly an Indian footpath in the days before the horse, now washed and worn deeper than a tall man's head. The passage was narrow, steep, littered with rocks, and with many switchbacks. But the high walls on either side would shelter anyone inside the trail from rifle fire from the compound. Any pursuers would have to come on foot. And it topped out less than a hundred yards from the north pass. Slocum could easily cover both the pass and the trail from his post on the crest of the basin rim.

Getting Sissy to the trail would be the biggest problem. From the far end of the compound, he and Meg would have to cross almost two hundred yards of open ground before reaching the mesquite and huisache thicket where the path began.

Jimmy had committed every turn, every switchback, every stone of the escape trail to memory. Even in the blackest night, he knew he could manage the climb out—provided nobody spotted them before they reached it and raised a yell. If they made it that far, they'd be under the protection of Slocum's rifles. The horses, including the dead Indian's spooky-looking albino, waited just below the rim of the pass. The animals were rested, grained, saddled, and ready.

Jimmy only wished he could have brought his rifle, in case they had to make a stand. But *peones* normally didn't carry rifles. So the .38-40 stayed behind. The only weapons he had were Slocum's sharp skinning knife, a two-foot-long hardwood club carved from the living limb of a scrub oak tree, and the .41 Lightning Colt tucked beneath his belt. He carried a dozen spare handgun cartridges in his pocket.

It would have to do. He'd never fired the double-action revolver at anything but a target. But he was comfortable in his own mind he wouldn't get the shakes if something went wrong and he had to use it. The handgun was a last resort anyway. The last thing they wanted was a gunshot to wake up the whole compound. The club and the knife would have to do.

Slocum had taught Jimmy how to use both—where to strike with the most effective results.

With the club, he had three targets, depending on which way the guard happened to be facing. The back of the neck just below the skull, where a blow would snap a man's spine as surely as a hangman's knot. If that wasn't possible, the side of the head above the ear. Not as likely to kill, but it would put a man down long enough. And if those targets weren't available, the bridge of the nose. With a hard enough swing, bone slivers would drive into the guard's brain. A miss of a couple inches would still hopefully leave him unconscious.

Jimmy had confidence in the short, heavy club. It felt reassuring to the hand.

The knife was a different matter. His blood still chilled at the fresh memory of the blood pumping from the Comanche's throat at the pass, of how long it took the man to die. If he had to use it and a quick slash of the throat wasn't available, he knew where to thrust. From a low angle upward beneath the left ribs into the heart. Even that was neither quick nor silent. The guard might still have time to yell out. And if Jimmy missed the heart, the man might be able to grab him while others came running. That would be the end of James Daniel Forrest. And with his death would go Meg's only chance of escape.

The woman who brought the food worried Jimmy more than the guard. He would have only seconds to duck into the house and put her down before she could yell an alarm. She was a big, stout woman. It had to be done that way, though. Only when the big woman came was the door left unlocked for a few minutes.

He refused to let his mind dwell on all the things that could go wrong. As Slocum had said, a man who went into a fight thinking he was whipped was whipped before it started.

When they reached the top of the pass and the horses, they could open up some distance on anybody who came after them. With Slocum's .44-95 Peabody, Winchester, and revolvers, distance was their short-range ace in the hole. The one thing that would save them in the long run was the horses. Shiloh was sure to send men after them. If they had a big enough start, it wouldn't matter. Nobody was likely to catch them in a horse race.

Jimmy's heart jumped as a shadowy form drew near. A soft mutter of Spanish with an uplift at the end, like a question, fell on his ears. He didn't speak the language. He waved a hand casually in what he hoped was a sleepy-looking greeting. It must have been enough. The Mexican ambled past and disappeared into the stables. The tremble of Jimmy's fingers gradually subsided along with his heart rate as he studied his next move.

It was going to be touchy. He had to get word to Meg they were coming, and do so without attracting attention from the guard posted outside.

Men were creatures of habit. That worked in Jimmy's favor. The guards had fallen into the routine of standing beside the west window. That left the east window unguarded. Once in place, the guards seldom moved. Just leaned against the wall and waited for the next guard to relieve them. Sometimes they even napped or drank from a bottle they'd brought to relieve the boredom of the job.

Jimmy became aware of a strange sensation, a weird calmness that seemed to drape itself over his shoulders. His heartbeat slowed to steady and normal, the sweat dried from his palms, his senses took on a sharper edge, and he wasn't afraid any longer. He didn't understand it, but it felt good. He'd ask Slocum about it some time.

He glanced at the stars again. In another half hour or so, he would have to slip up to the unguarded east window and tell Meg. He could only hope she was still a light sleeper. He shifted the club to a more comfortable position and let his head drop, feigning sleep.

Meg awoke from a fitful doze, her skin soaked in sweat and tingling. She lay still for a moment, waiting for the squirmy feeling in her belly to subside. It didn't.

She had no idea what had brought on the sudden attack of anxiety and twanging nerves, the sense that something was about to happen. She gave up the idea of trying to go back to sleep, dressed silently, and chanced a quick glimpse of the guard outside the west window. The man leaned against the wall, hat tipped forward over his eyes, his breathing deep and steady.

Meg found herself drawn to the rack of firewood as if by some unseen force. She slipped her hand beneath the rack, not even bothering to worry that a scorpion might be there. The sharpened stick still lay in its place of concealment.

She pulled it out, tested its point with her thumb, then slipped it between her breasts and beneath her left armpit. The crude weapon's touch against her ribs seemed reassuring. She stood, her skin still tingling in the cool darkness of her prison home.

She took a tentative step toward the bed, then stopped. Something—she didn't know what—pulled her toward the east window. She stood against the wall alongside the barred but unshuttered window open to the night air, her heart pounding.

A faint scuffle from outside sent her heart into her throat.

"Sissy?"

The soft whisper, the familiar but deeper voice, hit her in the heart.

"Meg, are you in there?"

"Jimmy—it can't be—is that you?"

"It's me, Sissy. I've come to get you out of here. There's a friend waiting for us with saddled horses up on the rim."

"Jimmy, you can't! It's too dangerous!"

"Be quiet and listen, Meg. I'm coming for you when the woman brings breakfast. Be ready. I can't talk any longer. Too chancy."

Meg's heart finally came down from her throat. She desperately wanted to yell out, "Jimmy, no! You'll just get yourself killed!"

But the words didn't come. A yell would get him killed for sure. A hundred questions swirled in her brain, questions that would have to wait. But mostly, her mind focused on one thing: Her little brother had followed, somehow, all the way from Nebraska. He was here, inside the compound. It wasn't possible for a kid his age to do that. But he was here. And he was going to try it. Even if it meant capture or death.

For a moment, she thought it was all a dream, that she still lay asleep on the bed. But she knew she was fully awake. And more frightened than she had been in her entire life, even on that horrible day up in Nebraska.

Despite the fear that knotted her insides—for Jimmy, not for herself—a surge of love and admiration warmed her heart. She should have known, she chided herself, that Jimmy would somehow find her. The boy didn't realize it, perhaps, but he had inherited a stubbornness of will from his father. A streak of stubbornness that would most likely get him killed. She edged closer to the window, trying to peer past the bars. She saw nothing. But Jimmy had been there. It had been no apparition.

A voice from the west window jolted her, deepened the chill already in her bones.

It was Bill Smith's voice.

"I'll take over, Chuck. Grub's almost ready."

"Much obliged, Brazos." The answer was groggy, laden with the remnants of sleep. "Reckon I could use a bait. My belly thinks my throat's cut."

Bootsteps scuffled away into the distance. Meg strode silently to the west window. Smith's profile was faint against the distant glow from a single window—the kitchen of Shiloh's building in the quadrangle.

After a moment, Meg said softly, "Bill—"

"I had to tell you, Meg," his hoarse whisper interrupted, "the Apache, Scar, will be here by sundown today—"

"It doesn't matter," Meg broke in, desperation in her tone. "You've got to get out of here, Bill. Get away from this house."

For a moment, there was no answer. Then Smith said, "Something's up, isn't it?"

Meg hesitated, torn between the need to save the young man's life and a reluctance to trust him. "Yes," she finally said. "Go now. I don't want to see you get killed."

"What is it, Meg? For God's sake, you have to tell me. Otherwise, I can't help you."

"Help me?"

"I've done some hard thinking, Meg. I can't let that damned Apache get his hands on you. I told you earlier I couldn't help, not then. Now, I have to."

"You can't, Bill. If you stay here, you'll get killed—and I can't stop it now." She drew a deep breath. She had to trust him if she were to save his life. "I'm leaving here. At breakfast."

She heard the quick intake of breath through the open window. "How?"

"There isn't time to explain. There's only minutes left. Please go. Now. Before it's too late. I—can't let you die, Bill."

"It doesn't matter." His whispered words took on an urgency of their own. "Dammit, Meg, you have to let me do this. For once in my life, let me do just one good thing. One thing to prove to myself that I'm a man. If I get killed, it won't matter. Everybody dies sometime."

Meg chewed her lower lip for a moment, then told him help was coming for her. "My brother," she ended softly.

Smith stood for a few heartbeats, still staring into the distance. Over his shoulder, Meg saw the back door of the kitchen swing open, the blocky form stepping though carrying a small lantern and a tray.

"You'll need a diversion, something to keep their attention away from here for a spell," he said softly. "I'll take care of it." And then he was gone. One moment he was there, the next he wasn't.

Doubt and fear swirled in Meg's mind. Had she sacrificed her brother and herself by trusting an outlaw? Even one who didn't fit the normal mold?

There was no time left to worry. She pulled the pointed stick from beneath her dress and flattened herself against the wall, away from the hinges of the door.

Jimmy stood in the deep shadow of the east wall, momentarily confused. There was no sentry. It didn't make sense. The west window was always under guard. He thought he had caught sight of a dim figure striding away just moments before he rounded the corner of the east wall.

He glanced around. There was no sign of life except for the stocky woman approaching, a lantern swinging by her side. Jimmy pressed his shoulders against the rough adobe. The time to strike was after she had opened the padlock and stepped inside the door. Her back would be to him then.

He forced his tense muscles to relax as the scrape of a heavy key in a lock reached his ears, then a faint rasp of iron hinges as the door swung open. He took a tentative step—and heard a sudden grunt, a thud, a scuffle of feet, from inside.

He went through the door, the club already drawn back, ready to strike. The first thing he saw was his sister, her body thrust against the big woman. Something protruded from the woman's side; the light from the fallen lantern showed the big woman's mouth open, her right hand reaching for a knife at her belt.

Jimmy took a step to his left and swung the club with all his strength. The crack of neck bones snapping seemed louder than the blow itself. The big woman dropped like a stone on her side, mouth still open in the shout or scream that never formed. A bloody stick protruded from beneath her rib cage.

"Jimmy—" Meg said, breathing hard from the exertion of the struggle.

Jimmy reached for her wrist. "Come on, Meg! There's no time to talk now. We've got to move!"

He all but pulled her outside into the shadows, then closed the door and led Meg into the deeper shadows of the east side. As they passed the window where they had spoken earlier, Jimmy saw the light from the dropped lantern flicker and go out.

"Steady now, Meg," he whispered. She was barely visible in the predawn blackness. He squeezed her arm. "Grab the end of this blanket, so we don't get separated, and follow me. Walk slow, like we was just a young couple out for a walk."

"Jimmy, how—"

"Be quiet, Meg. The hardest part's yet to come. We can talk later. When we're out of here."

Past the northeastern corner of the quadrangle and stables waited the longest hundred-plus yards of Jimmy's life.

And dawn was breaking. Already, the darkness that had gripped the basin was giving way to a faint, gray light. He paused for a quick glance around. There were still no guards posted in this area, no one to be seen except an elderly Mexican woman shuffling toward a berry thicket, a pail in her hand.

Jimmy slipped the club he still carried beneath the makeshift serape, tucked it under his belt, and drew the .41 Colt. "Walk on my left side," he said to Meg. "Hold my arm, but real loose. If anybody comes after us, make a run for that thicket. See that rock shaped like a bull's head just above the thicket?"

"I see it." Meg's breathing had slowed; she had her wind back from the brief struggle with the big woman. She became aware of a sting at the base of her right hand. A splinter from the wooden stake. It was worth it, she thought; the feel of that piece of wood driving up under the woman's ribs remained fresh in her mind and muscles. That's for you, Carla, and all the others, she thought.

"That's where the trail up to the rim starts. If anybody sees us, I'll slow 'em down. You get up that trail as quick as you can." Jimmy drew a deep breath. "Ready?"

"Ready."

The slow, casual stroll toward the thicket seemed to Jimmy to take forever. The light grew stronger, brightening from its faint gray. They had to pass within twenty yards of the old woman carrying the bucket. She glanced up and stared at the two for a moment. Meg waved a cheerful greeting. Jimmy breathed a silent sigh as she went back to picking the wild berries.

They were within ten yards of the thicket when the first startled yelp sounded from the direction of the compound. Meg's grip tightened on his left arm.

"Steady now," Jimmy said. "It'll take 'em a minute or two to figure out what's going on." Still, he didn't breathe easier until the first few limbs of the mesquite thicket closed behind them. He turned, peered through the opening, and mouthed a soft curse.

Three men, led by a tall, thin man with only one arm, had left the compound, following their tracks. The second man in line was huge, well over six feet, and walked with a limp. Jimmy knew at a glance these were two of the men who had hit the ranch. He had tracked them too long not to know. He didn't recognize the third man.

"The one out front's called Ace," Meg whispered at his side, peering through the opening over Jimmy's shoulder. "The big one with the limp is Hank. They were in the bunch—"

"I know, Meg." Jimmy heard the tight rage in his own words. "I hope those two come after us. As long as they don't bring help. Come on. Let's get to the trail. Don't run. Save your wind and strength. It's a hard climb."

Jimmy glanced over the edge of the trail just before the wall grew over his head. His heart skidded. The skinny man and the big one still followed, but the third man hurried back toward the compound almost in a run.

Jimmy paused long enough to check the loads in the .41 Lightning, then reached for Meg's arm. "Let's go, Sissy. We've got some climbing to do, and every man in that camp's going to be after us—"

A sudden flash and boil of smoke and debris soared high over the compound; an instant later, a thunderous blast jarred the ground beneath Jimmy's feet. "What the hell?"

"It's Bill! The one called Brazos! He said he'd get their attention for us. He's blown the powder shed! My God, he's going to get killed—for us." Meg's words caught in her throat.

Jimmy glanced at her, confused. Why should she give a damn what happened to some outlaw? He let it pass. There wasn't time now. The two men on foot had reached the base of the game trail.

"There he is!" Meg pointed toward a lone horseman, headed in a long lope toward the milling remuda of horses south of the camp. "What's he—"

"Forget him, Meg," Jimmy snapped. "We've got troubles of our own. We've got to get up this trail."

The thunderous blast skittered the heavy coffee mug on the table, shaking the floor beneath Dunnigan's feet. It had come less than a second after Joaquin's startled yelp from the midhouse.

"What the hell?" Dunnigan came to his feet, toppling his chair backward with a clatter. He strapped on his cartridge belt, grabbed his rifle and hat, and was halfway to the front door when the panel suddenly flew open.

"Trouble, *Coronel!*" Joaquin said. "The magazine, she blows up. Donna is dead. The girl is gone."

Shiloh stood for a moment, stunned. "Dammit! There's no way that magazine blew by itself—and the girl sure as hell didn't get away on her own. Joaquin, saddle up and fetch the remuda. *Pronto!*"

"Brazos already goes for the horses."

"Then mount all the men you can from the horses in the stables. Tell Pedro to saddle my gray. I want that girl back. Where's that damn Comanche?"

Joaquin shrugged. "Nobody see him for days, Señor."

"Shit! That Injun's never around when he's needed. Don't just stand there, man! Move!" Dunnigan tugged on his cavalry-style campaign hat and followed as Joaquin scurried out the back toward the stables.

Thick, choking smoke, dust, and debris almost obscured his vision in the quadrangle. It had been a hell of a blast. A momentary break in the haze showed two bodies lying fifty feet or so from the rubble of the magazine, one almost cut in half, the other dragging himself by the elbows and screaming for help. Dunnigan ignored the downed men. A few losses didn't concern him.

He ducked inside the mid-house. Donna was dead. A crude makeshift wooden stake-stick slanted upward beneath her ribs. Her head flopped at a weird angle against her right shoulder. Dunnigan quickly searched the body. The key Donna always carried was missing. And the same key fit the padlocks on the magazines.

Joaquin and almost a dozen men were already in the saddle, Joaquin leading Dunnigan's gray, when he stepped outside.

"Tracks lead up toward the north rim, Señor. The girl and a small man's footprints. Ace and Hank follow them on foot."

Dunnigan grunted. At least somebody around here had some sense. He turned to the stable hand. "Pedro, when Brazos gets here with the remuda, mount up thirty men and send them after us. Tell Dutch I want all the others in defensive positions. He'll know what to do until I get back. *Sabe?*"

Pedro nodded vigorously. "*Sí, Coronel.*"

Dunnigan glared toward the north pass, only now beginning to catch the first rays of the sun. "Let's ride, men. Up the north pass, then fan out. They're on foot. If Hank and Ace don't get them, they won't be hard to track down. Don't kill the girl. I want that bitch back. I'll by God *give* her to Scar if I have to. She'll find out damn quick not to cross Shiloh Dunnigan. Let's ride."

●   ●   ●

Brazos checked his sorrel back to a quick trot as he neared the outlaw remuda. The horses milled and snorted nervously, still spooked by the massive explosion of the powder storehouse. The two night wranglers had their hands full keeping the horses from bolting. That would make his job easier.

Brazos's own ears still rang from the concussion of the blast. He slipped his old Schofield from its holster, thumbed back the hammer, and held the weapon down alongside his leg.

He didn't know either of the wranglers by sight. Somehow, that made it easier. A bay tried to break away from the remuda and head for the compound; Brazos reined his sorrel aside and turned the bay back. The near wrangler had closed to within a dozen yards.

"What happened back there?" the wrangler yelled.

Brazos lifted the Schofield and shot the man in the chest. He rammed spurs to the sorrel and charged the remuda, whooping and firing the six-gun in the air.

The already spooked horses panicked. As one, the whole remuda turned and stampeded toward the open south pass. Over the thunder of hooves, Brazos heard the angry buzz as a bullet whipped past his ear and the flat blast of a handgun sounded. The second wrangler, some fifty yards away, dismounted and knelt, steadying his revolver with an elbow braced against his knee.

Brazos swung his Schofield toward the kneeling man, pulled the trigger—and the hammer clicked against a spent cartridge.

Brazos saw the smoke from the handgun. A fist hammered into his right side. His hip felt cold. He reined the sorrel sharply toward the wrangler, put the animal into a dead run, and crouched low over the horse's neck. The wrangler's revolver cracked again. Brazos felt his horse flinch, almost go down; then the sorrel's shoulder and knee rammed into the wrangler, knocking him onto his back. The man's handgun spun away. He didn't move after he hit the ground.

Brazos spun the fading sorrel about, grabbed the trailing reins of the wrangler's chestnut, and pulled the walleyed animal alongside. Without dismounting, he swung from his saddle into the wrangler's rig a couple of strides before the sorrel went down, its hooves flailing feebly.

The pain hit Brazos then, a slight sting at first as he thumbed the barrel latch of the Schofield, dumped the spent cases from the top-break action, and reloaded on the run, letting the chestnut have its head as the animal raced toward the distant remuda. The pain turned sharp as Brazos snapped the Schofield's action shut. He holstered the weapon on the second try, freeing his right arm to grab the saddlehorn as a wave of nausea cramped his gut. He was losing strength fast.

He barely heard the hum of the slug past his ear, followed by the crack of a rifle. Another slug kicked dirt six feet in front of the chestnut. Brazos knew he was caught in a cross fire from the lookouts on each side of the south pass. There was nothing to do but ride. He kneed the chestnut into a zigzag run, trying to force his fuzzy brain not to repeat the pattern twice.

Half a dozen other slugs missed, one nicking the edge of his hat brim. Then he was out of rifle range, the chestnut pounding after the fleeing remuda.

He reined the winded horse back to a lope, then a trot. The south pass was well behind him now. He ground his teeth against the growing agony in his hip and side, and fought to focus his gaze, blink away the thin film of haze from his vision.

He looked back over his shoulder. There was no pursuit yet, but he knew there would be; Shiloh had to get those horses back. From here, Smith couldn't see the north pass, or the basin rim above. He could only hope that Meg would be able to make it to safety, somehow slip away from the men who would be after her.

The notion he had been fighting for weeks finally battled its way through his swirling brain. He could never have her. But he could die content, knowing that if she lived, he had helped save the life of the girl he had grown to love.

The thought that for the first time in his life he had done something worthwhile seemed to ease the growing agony a bit. Staying in the saddle required all his strength now. He knew he didn't have much time left.

10

Jimmy's leg muscles quivered and burned, threatening to fail him at any moment. He couldn't pull in enough air to fill his lungs, and his heart hammered in his chest. And they had made it only a third of the way up the deep, twisting game trail toward the top of the basin rim.

He knew they had to stop and catch their wind.

Meg, an arm's length in front of him, hadn't complained once. But he knew his sister was closer to collapse than he was; he could hear her gasps for air above his own ragged breathing. The thin-soled slippers she wore provided little protection from the rocks that littered the trail. Every step brought the threat of a twisted or broken ankle.

And he had underestimated the endurance of the one-armed man and the big one with the bad ankle. The two were gaining on them. It didn't seem possible, but it was happening. He could hear the scuffle of boots, the occasional grunt of exertion, when the trail doubled back almost upon itself until the pursuers and the pursued were within a few feet of each other, separated only by the steep, rocky walls flanking the path.

He didn't know what the distant gunshots to the south meant, or the dust cloud he had glimpsed through a notch in the wall. Or the shouts that carried faintly from the basin floor.

But he knew the two men after them were part of the gang that had killed his parents and raped his sister. And that he

136

wasn't going to get a better chance than now to take at least one of them down. He was tired of running, but not just from exhausted muscles.

He reached out and tugged at the tail of Meg's dress. Her face was flushed, chest heaving, when she half turned.

"Just up ahead—twenty feet or so," Jimmy said between gasps for air. "Narrow switchback to the right by that big rock. We'll stop there a minute and catch our wind."

"But—won't they—catch up to us?"

Jimmy fingered the butt of the .41 Lightning tucked in his belt. "I want the bastards to," he said.

Ten minutes later, Jimmy leaned against the left side of the steep, sharp turn that was so narrow a big man could barely pass. His chest still heaved, but his vision was clear, his hand steady. He heard the distant clatter of hooves, and guessed that riders were headed for the north pass. Straight into Slocum's rifle. That bunch was going to be busy for a while.

A footstep grated on stones just around the bend.

He glanced over his shoulder at Meg, putting the index finger of his left hand to his lips. At her wide-eyed nod, Jimmy raised the muzzle of the Lightning.

The one-armed man rounded the bend, his narrow chest heaving, his gaze downcast as he picked his way through the litter of fist-sized stones. His handgun was still holstered.

"Hello, Ace," Jimmy said softly. "Time to pay."

The one-armed man's head jerked up; his hand stabbed at the revolver at his hip. Jimmy squeezed the trigger. The soft-nosed .41 slug took the skinny man low in the chest. He grunted at the impact, but didn't go down. Ace's handgun was free of leather when Jimmy lined the sights of his .41 Lightning, taking his time as Slocum had taught him, and fired. The muzzle flash almost touched the man's throat. He dropped straight down like a sack of sugar falling from a wagon.

Jimmy knew the one-armed man was dead before he hit the ground. The .41 might not pack much punch at fifty yards, but from point-blank range it had plenty of wallop to bust a man's windpipe and tear through his spinal cord.

A moment's silence followed the gunshots. Then a call came from around the bend:

"Ace?"

"Your friend won't be rapin' and killin' no more, Hank," Jimmy called back. "Come on, damn you—if you got the guts to settle up for what you done up on the Republican."

There was no immediate answer. Jimmy knelt and picked up the one-armed man's revolver. It was a Remington Army chambered for the .46 Short rimfire. Two down, four to go, Jimmy thought. He felt no qualms or regrets, only satisfaction, that the man named Ace had finally paid the price. He stripped the cartridge belt from the dead man's waist, tossed it over a shoulder, and handed the old Remington to Meg.

"You know how to use this, Sissy," Jimmy whispered. "Use it if you have to. Got your wind back?"

She didn't look directly at Jimmy. A muscle twitched in her jaw as she glared at the dead man. "You finished the job Mother started," she said softly. "She got a slug into the bastard that day. I'm feeling much better now."

Jimmy glanced up at the basin rim. It seemed a mile away. He cocked his head, listening. He heard nothing from beyond the bend in the trail. The big man called Hank wasn't in a rush to walk into the same ambush that killed his friend.

Jimmy said, "All right, let's go."

At his sniper's perch at the rim of the north pass, Slocum grunted in satisfaction as the familiar flat blasts of Jimmy's Lightning reached his ears.

There had been no return fire. The two pistol shots told Slocum at least one of Shiloh Dunnigan's men had most likely ridden his last raid. The kid learned well. The faint, nagging worry that Jimmy might not be able to pull off the night raid was behind Slocum now. The light had been good enough that he had seen the two distant figures reach the questionable cover of the mesquite thicket at the base of the game trail, followed shortly by two of Dunnigan's men. Most likely, Jimmy still had one man left to deal with.

Slocum now was sure Jimmy could handle it. He silently chided himself for doubting the boy's ability in the first place. Sometimes youth was an advantage. Young men didn't realize

when something was damn near impossible to do. They just
did it.

Besides that, Slocum still had enough to worry about.

Most pressing, at the moment, was the knot of horsemen
approaching the trail at the bottom of the pass. A few more
minutes and they would be in range of the Peabody. In the
back of his mind, though, Slocum couldn't help but wonder
at other unexplained developments of the past few hours.

The dust cloud visible through the spyglass from the look-
out point just before sundown yesterday, miles to the southwest, likely would be the Apache, Scar, and his warrior band.

The second, and considerably larger, dust cloud, far to the
east-southeast, Slocum couldn't explain. He had learned to always be wary of the unknown. It could be a herd of cattle on
the move. Or more renegades bound for the Shiloh basin. If
the latter, it meant more trouble. It took a lot of men and
horses to raise a dust that big.

Then there was the massive blast when the powder magazine went up, and the lone rider who had stampeded the Shiloh
horses. Slocum didn't know who he was, only that it looked
like the man had taken a slug in the process. Curious. Somebody had helped them, intentionally or by accident. Slocum
pushed the thought aside. A man took his help—and his good
breaks—when he found them. Along with the bad.

It was about time to go to work.

The riders from Shiloh were heading up the pass trail now,
their horses at a lunging lope as the slope steepened. There
had been a dozen of them, but two had reined off toward the
stampeded horse herd.

Slocum was ready. Nine cartridges for the .44-95 lay near
the receiver of the single-shot rifle. He already had racked the
sliding notch of the rear tang sight up to the five-hundred-yard
bar. His Winchester waited within easy reach, the spare Peacemaker from his saddlebag tucked under his belt at the small
of his back.

He wasn't short of firepower. If he didn't consider the odds.
All he could do about that was to cut those odds some.

As the riders neared the fallen tree trunk Slocum had picked
as his range marker at the widest spread of the pass, Dirk

Dunnigan dropped back to the middle of the pack. Slocum wasn't surprised. Cowards might lead if there was no potential danger to themselves out front. Otherwise, they followed. Or just hid out until the danger had passed. It didn't matter. Slocum wanted to take Shiloh face-to-face if possible.

He thumbed back the Peabody's hammer, drew a deep breath, and picked his target. The sights settled on the lead rider, a thick-shouldered man on a stocky bay. Slocum exhaled slowly and squeezed the trigger.

The muzzle blast of the Peabody hammered his ears as the buttstock slammed against his shoulder. Almost a full second later, the big man on the bay tumbled over the rump of his horse as if hit by a cannon ball, his hat still hanging in midair.

Slocum worked the action of the Peabody, and had another round chambered before the startled yelps from the horsemen reached his ears. He picked a second target, the X formed by the crossed cartridge bandoliers on a small man's chest, mentally adjusted for the slightly shorter range, and squeezed. The rider spun from the saddle and fell beneath the hooves of two other horses close behind. One of the horses stumbled over the body and fell, spilling its rider. The man rolled to his feet and ran for cover, diving into a shallow wash before Slocum could reload.

The charge abruptly broke. The remaining horsemen spurred for the trees and rocks alongside the pass. Dunnigan was the first to rein aside. Slocum muttered a curse. He hadn't had time to reload and drop Dunnigan's horse before a clump of junipers swallowed the outlaw leader.

One rider's mount panicked, started bucking, and dumped the man thirty feet from a rockfall. Slocum put a slug through the man's spine. The rider twitched and lay still.

Slocum saw the puff of smoke from behind a pine tree as he reloaded. The slug from the outlaw's rifle fell well short of the basin rim. Repeating rifles didn't have the reach for a shot of nearly a quarter mile.

A ragged volley of lead kicked dirt fifty yards down the slope from Slocum's vantage point. He ignored the harmless gunfire, waiting for a target. He figured he had another six or seven shots before the Peabody's accuracy began to go from black powder fouling—

Slocum winced as a heavy slug snarled past just overhead, followed by the throaty roar of a big-bore rifle. One of the shooters had a long-range buffalo gun. A Sharps Fifty, judging from the sound of the muzzle blast. And the bastard could shoot; that big slug had been a bit close for comfort.

The stakes had just gone up in this game.

Slocum had to take the buffalo gunner down before the rifleman nailed him. It was a challenge Slocum had faced before, two long-range snipers, one in blue, one in gray, jockeying for the final, killing shot.

But this time there was a complication.

Other men would be working their way up toward him. They would have reinforcements on the way soon. They would have reinforcements on the way soon. And Slocum had to hold this pass until Jimmy and his sister were in the clear. . . .

The heavy blasts of Slocum's Peabody pumped new strength into Jimmy's quavering leg muscles. They had to reach the top of the rim, then the pass, before Slocum was overrun.

He glanced once toward the sound of the big rifle and the ragged volley of lighter cracks from outlaw rifles, but the walls of the deep, twisting trail hid the crest of the pass from view.

Jimmy could hear Meg's labored breathing over his own gasps. She stumbled more often now, partly from exhausted climbing muscles and partly from the light slippers that gave her little grip on the rocky trail, and even less protection from the sharp stones and sticks littering the path. And he also heard the irregular scuffle of big boots from behind them.

The big man called Hank wouldn't quit. Jimmy had counted on that.

Beyond the next steep switchback waited a surprise that should give the cripple enough of a shock that Jimmy could get a good crack at him. Jimmy's pounding heart skipped a beat at Meg's sharp grunt of pain; she sank to her knees, her left arm reaching back toward her ankle. He knelt at her side.

"What is it, Sissy?"

"Foot—think I tore something," she gasped. "Felt a pop in my instep."

The scuffling sound behind them was closer now, just beyond the last turn. If they were caught here, on this short, straight stretch—he wouldn't let himself complete the thought.

"Can you walk?"

Meg grimaced, her gasps for air coming through clenched teeth. "I don't know." Her gaze caught his. The expression in her eyes was a mix of hopelessness and love. "Go on, Jimmy. Save yourself. I'm not worth it—"

"The hell you aren't." Jimmy's words held a tight, hard edge. "Dammit, Meg, we've been apart too long and you've been through too much. I'm sure not gonna leave you behind now, and I won't let you quit on me." He slipped his left arm around her waist and all but lifted her to her feet. "All we've got to do is get around that next bend. We can make it."

Another volley of rifle fire sounded from the pass rim as Jimmy half carried Meg toward the sharp switchback ahead. The blast of a big rifle that wasn't Slocum's Peabody echoed through the basin. One of the outlaws had a buffalo gun. Slocum could be in bigger trouble than *they* were.

Carrying most of Meg's weight, slight though it was, Jimmy thought his heart would burst and his legs fail before they finally reached the abrupt switchback. As they turned the corner he heard Meg's startled gasp.

Twenty feet away, a man's head rested on a rock ledge, its eyes and mouth open in a death grimace. Blackish stains from Injun Tom's dried blood darkened the rock shelf.

Jimmy dragged Meg five yards past the grisly trophy, pushed her against a solid rock wall, and drew the .41 Lightning from his waistband. Meg still held the one-armed man's old rimfire Remington in her right fist. The scuffling sounds were almost on them now, just beyond the last bend they'd taken.

"That head's our trump card, Meg," Jimmy said between gasps for air. "Maybe it'll get his attention for a second. From this range, I can't miss." He lifted the Colt. The bird's-head grips were slick beneath his sweaty palm, and the sights trembled a bit. Jimmy tried to steady his nerves. They were so damn close to the top of the rim now—

The huge man stepped around the bend, a six-gun in his massive right hand. His eyes went wide as his gaze locked on the Comanche's severed head.

Jimmy pulled the trigger. A puff of dust flew from the big man's shirtfront, but he didn't go down; he just looked even more surprised. Jimmy didn't fight the recoil of the .41, just let the weapon drop back into line of its own weight, and fired again. Another puff of dust—and Hank still stood, the revolver in his hand rising. Jimmy fired twice more, as fast as he could pull the trigger of the double-action Lightning. The hammer fell with a dull click on a spent round when he pulled the trigger again. He had emptied the chamber, four shots had hit their mark, and still the black bore of Hank's handgun swung toward him.

"Down, Jimmy!" Meg yelled.

Jimmy dropped to his knees. An instant later, the muzzle blast of the .46 Short pounded painfully against his ears as Meg fired over his shoulder. A dark spot bloomed at the base of the big man's throat; the muzzle of the handgun in the big fist wavered, then began to drop. Blood spurted from the neck wound. Meg fired again. Dust kicked from the big man's shirt directly over the heart.

Jimmy could only stand and watch as Hank struggled to lift his revolver. Blood already covered the front of his shirt. He lifted a bleary gaze toward Meg.

"Didn't—think you—had it in you, girl," he muttered, his voice gurgling through the blood in his lungs and throat. Then he sank to his knees, the revolver dropping from his hand. A couple of seconds later, Hank toppled forward, facedown.

Jimmy twisted to glance at Meg, his ears ringing from the muzzle blasts. She still gripped Ace's big Remington Army in both hands, the hammer pulled back for another shot, her face pale and lips clenched into a thin line. The muzzle of the Remington never wavered.

"Thanks, Sissy," Jimmy said as he fumbled to reload the Lightning. "That man was a tough son of a bitch. Four slugs from a .41 Colt and it was like he didn't even feel 'em. I thought he had us for sure. You okay?"

Meg nodded grimly. "He's still moving. Step back, Jimmy. I don't want to deafen you, if I haven't already." When he was clear, Meg carefully aimed the Remington. "This is something I've been looking forward to, you big bastard. This is from Mother and me. Time to pay," she said to the twitching form in the trail. She squeezed the trigger.

The .46-caliber slug slammed through the top of Hank's battered hat into his brain. The big man stopped moving.

Jimmy shoved the final round into his Lightning. He took the Remington from Meg, ejected the empties, and reloaded the weapon from Ace's cartridge belt around his shoulder.

Meg's expression was almost peaceful, but the hate still burned in her eyes. "These two—Hank and Injun Tom—were the worst of the lot, next to Shiloh," she said. "By God, they'll never rape or kill again. Who killed the Comanche?"

"Slocum. And me. Well, both of us."

"Did it take a while for him to die? Did he suffer?"

"Some," Jimmy said.

"He didn't hurt enough. Whose idea was it to cut his head off?"

"Mine," Jimmy said. "Thought we could maybe use it. Looks like I was right. How's the foot?"

"Still hurts. I think I can walk, with help."

The sound of gunfire at the mouth of the pass came more frequently now. "Let's go, Meg. I think Slocum could use some help."

Slocum ignored the lighter rifle slugs, despite the fact that they were inching closer to his makeshift shooting pit on the pass rim.

The gunners with carbines and repeating rifles were flanking him, edging up the timber and brush lining the sides of the pass. He would deal with them later.

At the moment, his attention was wholly focused on one man. The shooter with the long-range Sharps. Slocum mentally tipped his hat to the rifleman as a big slug nicked the rock a foot to the left of his shoulder and whined off into the distance. The man could shoot. But he wasn't a trained sniper, and there was more to such a contest than just being able to put a piece of lead where it needed to be.

The man had made a mistake.

He'd fallen into a pattern. That last shot had been as predictable as sunrise. And the man who survived a long-range rifle match was the man who did the unexpected. The shooter was a touch over three hundred yards away now. His pattern was to fire one shot, then bolt from that cover to the next rockfall or tree up the side of the hill, looking for a higher and better angle to the target.

Now Slocum knew where the shooter would be headed after the next round, a clump of boulders fifty feet higher up than the spot where the last powder smoke boil had bloomed.

Slocum was down to a couple of rounds for the Peabody, but the weapon hadn't yet fouled so badly that its accuracy suffered, at least from this range. He lowered the rear sight ladder to the three-hundred-yard notch and shifted the weapon slightly, its muzzle pointed toward an opening between the trees and rocks. The shooter would have to cross that open spot to get to the boulders higher up.

It would have to be a quick shot at a moving target; the .44-95 slug would take nearly half a second to cover that range. Slocum had made tougher shots before. He thumbed back the Peabody's hammer and waited.

During a lull in the shooting, Slocum heard a voice call, "Hey, Ferg! Reckon we got him? He ain't shot back in near ten minutes!"

"Don't take no chances—"

A quick series of handgun shots, four of them the distinctive, flat thump of a .41 Colt and two more, then a third a couple of seconds later, from a weapon Slocum couldn't identify, sounded from near the top of the game trail to his right. He could only hope Jimmy hadn't run into something he couldn't handle. There wasn't time to worry on it now.

Slocum saw the muzzle flash, the boil of powder smoke, felt the air crack as a heavy slug hummed within inches of his left ear, then heard the Sharps' muzzle blast. The shooter bolted from cover and started across the clearing at a crouching run. Slocum instinctively calculated the lead needed on the moving target and stroked the trigger. Half a heartbeat later, the running man sprawled forward, face-down, a long rifle sliding from limp hands. He didn't move.

Slocum grunted in satisfaction. That sharpshooter wouldn't be a problem now. The man had been dead or dying as soon as the Peabody slug had hit him. Slocum reloaded the single-shot, put it at his side, and picked up his .44-40 Winchester.

"All right, boys," he muttered aloud, "you want to dance, let's play the music."

For several long minutes, the firing stopped. Slocum could all but sense the confusion among the surviving members of Shiloh's mounted party.

In the distance at the far south end of the basin, Slocum saw a horseman spurring toward the buildings of Shiloh, waving his hat. It was one of the men who had gone after the stampeded horses, but the way he was riding told Slocum that bringing back mounts was the farthest thing from the rider's mind.

Beyond the south pass, a dust cloud—a big one—rose almost straight up in the nearly still air. Slocum didn't think Scar's band would raise that kind of dust.

A hundred yards to Slocum's right, a man in the garb of a *vaquero* showed his head and shoulder from behind a tree trunk. Slocum fired, hardly noticing the light recoil of the .44-40 against a shoulder numbed by the pounding of the Peabody. The *vaquero* yelped in pain, dropped his rifle, and ducked back behind the tree. A slug kicked dirt near Slocum's head. Two thirds of the way up the mountain to Slocum's left, smoke drifted from beneath a low-slung juniper. Slocum drove a round into the smoke, heard a startled yelp, but sensed the quick shot had been nothing more than a near-miss.

"Jackson!" Dunnigan yelled, still out of sight in the stand of pines.

"He's down, Colonel!" someone yelled back.

"Taylor?"

"Yeah?"

"Get back down to Shiloh! Tell Dutch to get twenty more men up here! Move, man! Covering fire!"

Slocum ducked his head below the edge of the rim as a volley of lead raked the lip of the basin. It was defensive shooting, blind trigger-yanking designed to cover a retreat. Slocum didn't attempt to return fire. It wasn't worth the risk of catching a wild slug.

The firing stopped. A man on a sorrel horse spurred toward the distant buildings. Slocum instinctively reached for the Peabody, then realized the range was too great for a shot at a moving target from a weapon already fouled by black powder and lead residue.

He glanced toward the pines where Dunnigan's shout had come from. At least now he knew where the bastard was.

"Corporal Dunnigan!" Slocum yelled. In the sudden quiet, voices carried well in the still air. He knew Dunnigan had heard. "No use getting any more of your men killed! You're such a big war hero, come up here yourself! You'll get a fair chance! Except you'll be facing a man, not shooting unarmed prisoners in the back!"

There was no answer. Slocum wasn't surprised. He hadn't expected the man to take the bait. But the challenge would maybe put some doubt in the minds of Dunnigan's followers.

The echoes of Slocum's call faded as an almost serene quiet settled over the battleground at the pass. For several minutes, nothing moved except the rustle of pine needles in the freshening breeze from the north. The eerie silence wasn't new to Slocum. It had happened many times during the war, and in civilian battles afterward—

The grind of gravel beneath a boot behind him and to his right snapped Slocum's head around.

A slender, dark-skinned man in a sombrero stood little more than ten yards away, the muzzle of a handgun already centered on Slocum. Slocum knew he had no chance to twist around, bring his own rifle into play, and take the man down before the outlaw could squeeze the trigger. He braced himself for the shock of a bullet.

A double slap of lead on flesh and an almost simultaneous blast of two handguns lifted the little Mexican onto his toes, the rifle muzzle dropping; Slocum could see the shock and disbelief on the gunman's face. The outlaw raised a hand halfway to his back, then toppled forward on his face.

Seconds later, Jimmy and a young blond woman stepped into view. Wisps of powder smoke curled from the .41 Lightning in Jimmy's hand and the big Remington in the girl's fist.

"Much obliged, partner," Slocum said. "Keep your heads down. A couple of those men down there can shoot. You two all right?"

Jimmy nodded, his chest heaving from exertion. "Meg, meet Slocum. Tell you about him later."

Meg cast a quick glance at Slocum, then glowered at the Mexican's corpse. "Joaquin. Injun Tom's friend. He was one of the bunch that came to the ranch that day."

"Then the bunch is thinnin' out in a hurry," Jimmy said in satisfaction. "Reckon they ain't but two of 'em left." A slug slapped against a rock a yard from Jimmy's shoulder. "Reckon we best mount up and get the hell out of here, Slocum. There's lots of men—and I mean *lots* of men—comin'. I seen 'em when Meg and me stopped to get our wind at the top of the rim. Half of 'em already lined up on the west side, just out of sight behind the rim. Another bunch headed up on this side. And it ain't gonna be long till they get here."

Slocum lifted an eyebrow. "How many would you guess?"

"Maybe six, seven hundred. Maybe a thousand." Jimmy instinctively reached out to grasp Meg's forearm. "Must be that renegade *commandante*'s men. They got cannons with 'em. Little ones. I seen half a dozen flags flyin' and they're wearin' uniforms. We got to get out now!"

The whirl of confusion in Slocum's mind suddenly snapped into clarity. If he was right, it would explain the milling and obvious confusion going on in the town below ever since the rider had spurred in from the south waving his hat and yelling. And why men were frantically saddling what few horses had been left behind or caught after the stampede.

Hope surged in Slocum's chest. "Jimmy, think on it a minute. Say you were a renegade *commandante* coming to hook up with Dunnigan. Would you split your force and surround the very army you intended to join? Wouldn't you just ride straight in from the south pass?"

Jimmy's brow furrowed in thought. "Reckon I would. Makes more sense. Unless I planned to bushwhack my partner and take over the whole shebang."

Slocum winced. "A possibility," he conceded.

"What's it all mean, Slocum? What do you thinks goin' on?"

"I think, my friend, that Don Viejo's message may have gotten through some Mexican skulls. If I'm right, today may see the end of Shiloh Dunnigan's big plans."

"And if you're wrong, Mr. Slocum?" Meg asked softly.

"It will be the last mistake I ever make." Slocum shifted his gaze back to Jimmy. "How long would you guess it will take before the men coming up on this side get into position?"

"Half hour maybe. Not more than that."

Slocum ignored the rifle slug that buzzed overhead. "Jimmy, bring me my saddlebags. Then you and Meg mount up and ride like hell. Just in case I'm wrong."

"What are you gonna do, Slocum?"

"Stay right here. At least as long as I can. I've got to hold this pass until the Mexican army gets into position. Now, go! Both of you!"

Jimmy and Meg strode away, but a few minutes later they returned. Jimmy carried both his and Slocum's saddlebags and one canvas pack. Meg, limping and wincing with each step, had three canteens cradled in one arm and Jimmy's .22 single-shot rifle in the other.

"What the hell's this about?" Slocum snapped. "I told you two to get out of here. I'll catch up with you later."

Jimmy shook his head. "I ain't leavin' you now, Slocum. We done rode too far together. Meg and me's gonna help you hold this pass, and don't go fussin' on it. You'll need all the help you can get." He tossed a leather pouch and a cartridge box to Slocum.

"Better run a quick patch or two through that Peabody," Jimmy added. "She's probably fouled bad by now. You got a dozen rounds left for it." Jimmy crouched beside Slocum, his .38-40 crooked in an elbow, and stared toward the settlement below. Slocum swabbed the fouling from the Peabody's barrel and chamber as best he could. The girl had stretched out on her belly at Jimmy's right, a box of .22 cartridges open beside her.

Slocum said, "Meg, I'd feel better if you stayed with the horses. You'd be safer. There'll likely be a lot of lead flying up here soon."

"Save your wind, Slocum," Jimmy said. "I couldn't talk her out of it, so don't figure you can. She gets downright stubborn sometimes."

"Jimmy's right, Mr. Slocum," Meg said. "I'm staying right here. We leave together or we don't leave at all."

Slocum heard fear and dread in her words. But he also heard determination and a touch of anger. Slocum's earlier hunch had been right. The girl had sand.

"Slocum," Jimmy said quietly, "if you ain't done with that Peabody now, you better hurry it up. There's about twenty men on horseback and about that many afoot comin' straight at us."

11

Slocum took his time loading the Peabody, his fingers moving instinctively as he studied the mob boiling from the stronghold below.

It was obvious the men weren't coming for a fight. Their handguns were holstered, rifles sheathed. They were running for their lives.

A flash of light on the west rim of the basin caught Slocum's eye. The light winked twice, paused again, then blinked on and off several more times.

Jimmy had seen it too.

"What's that light, Slocum?"

"Heliograph," Slocum said casually. "Sunlight flashed from a mirror. Armies—and Indians sometimes—use it to communicate over distances or terrain where they can't use runners."

"What'd it say?"

"Can't be sure without knowing the code of whoever's using it, but that series of flashes is more or less universal among organized armies. If I read it right, it said something to the effect that the troops are in position."

Jimmy glanced over his shoulder. The sun now stood almost two hours high in the east; a slice of the west side of the basin floor already was in full sunlight.

"They can't signal but one way with the sun where it's at, can they?" he asked.

"It can work both ways. You just use two mirrors, one to catch the sun's rays and flash them onto the signal mirror for relay." Slocum pointed a finger at the west rim. "See the washes of light just on the top? That's signals coming from this side. Unless I'm still reading it wrong, that was the signal for a half hour."

"Regular Mexican army?"

Slocum racked the Peabody's tang sight back up to eight hundred yards and pulled back the hammer. "Those men down there wouldn't be running from friendlies, partner." He shifted his gaze toward the basin. The horsemen had opened up a considerable lead on the men on foot. A few more yards and the lead riders would be in comfortable range of the Peabody.

Beyond the dust raised by the men charging his way, Slocum saw another group, maybe forty, running toward the south pass. And still, rifles bristled from walls and roofs of the town below. Must have been better than a couple hundred men down there when this show opened, he thought. He couldn't do anything about the others. Just the ones who were closing in on them.

"Party's about to open here," Slocum said to Jimmy. "You and Meg set up behind those boulders on the right side of the pass. Pick a spot where you can shoot without offering anybody a target. Wait until they get in range before you open up, then make every shot count. We've got to stand our ground here as long as we can, and hope it's long enough."

"Can we hold that long?"

"We have no choice, Jimmy. We don't want any of those guns behind us. We hold as long as we can, then get to the horses and ride like hell. Now, get Meg and yourself settled in. And watch behind you—some of them might be able to flank us when the fight gets hot and heavy."

Slocum rested the forearm of the big rifle across the jacket stuffed into the notch in the rocks that formed his shooting rest. "You and Meg keep your heads down. I'd sure hate to lose either or both of you."

Jimmy crabbed away, keeping close to the ground, and steered Meg into the jumble of rocks at Slocum's right. If the boy was scared, he didn't let it show, Slocum thought with a quiet warmth of pride tinged by more than a touch of worry. He couldn't let anything happen to Jimmy and his sister. Not now.

He settled the sights of the Peabody on the lead rider. If he'd had more firepower—say a full company of crack infantry troops—he'd have waited until they could loose a volley at close range. But he didn't have the luxury of setting up a full-scale ambush. He'd have to settle for giving this bunch something to think about.

Slocum realized that several minutes had passed since any of Dunnigan's men on the slope below had fired at them. Curious, he thought. If I had reinforcements on the way, I'd at least lay down a covering fire—

"Sit tight, men!" Dunnigan's yell sounded somewhat muffled from the cover of the pine motte. "The boys are on the way! We'll get the bastard up there now!"

"Maybe," Slocum muttered softly to himself, "but it's going to cost the hell out of you, Dunnigan." He stroked the trigger.

More than a second after the muzzle blast and seven hundred yards downrange, the lead horseman's body snapped back over the cantle of his saddle.

Slocum heard a startled yelp from a short distance downslope; then a couple of rifle shots kicked shards from the boulders he lay behind. He reloaded. The approaching horsemen hadn't broken stride when the lead rider went down. Those were some mighty scared hombres down there, Slocum thought as he lined the sights, squeezed, and emptied another saddle.

Jimmy's .38-40 cracked, bringing a squeal of pain and shock from close by. Dunnigan's first bunch was thinning out fast, Slocum thought. He didn't find much comfort in the notion. If those men on the trail kept coming, they'd overrun the defenders. Slocum, Jimmy, and Meg had the sun at their backs and good cover. It wouldn't be enough against that many men.

Slocum gritted his teeth and shot the horse from under the man who now rode in the lead. Two horses crowded close to the animal's rump stumbled over the downed bay and fell, spilling their riders.

The approaching outlaws seemed to suddenly realize they were under fire; they instinctively checked mounts, pulled rifles or handguns, and for a moment milled in confusion. They had closed to within three hundred yards of the rim. Slocum fired again, muttered a curse as the slug missed, and reloaded, wishing to hell somebody would come up with a long-range, big-bore rifle that held more than one cartridge at a time.

The survivors of Dunnigan's first bunch opened up on the rim now. Slocum counted only four rifles.

Beyond the milling horsemen, the men on foot sprinted as a group off to Slocum's left toward the cover of the timber and rocks along the side of the pass. At least he'd slowed them down. But in the process, he'd made the pass tougher to defend. The men on foot would work their way up into rifle range. Slocum didn't know how long they could hold when that happened.

A slug buzzed over Slocum's head; another spanged off the rocks behind which Jimmy and Meg crouched. Slocum ignored the brief spurt of rifle fire and waited for a clear target. He settled on one of the outriders, a man on a blue roan spurring toward the rim wall to Slocum's right, four others close behind. His finger tightened on the trigger—and eased as a flash of motion flickered in the stand of pines below and to his left.

Through a narrow break in the trees, Slocum saw Dunnigan had mounted. The outlaw leader turned his horse back down the slope toward the settlement below. No, you don't, you bastard, Slocum thought as he shifted the Peabody's muzzle. This time you don't run. Dunnigan's horse broke from the pine motte. Slocum put a .44-95 slug into the animal's shoulder. The horse went down.

Dunnigan kicked free of the stirrups and scrambled back into the pines before Slocum could get off another shot. At least now he wasn't going anywhere, Slocum thought grimly. It sort of made up for the queasy feeling in his gut at having to shoot horses. It wasn't their fault. Horses didn't carry guns.

The spasmodic firing picked up; most of the slugs fell short of the basin rim, but Slocum knew they would be in big trouble soon. The surviving gunmen on the trail below had made it to cover.

He thought he heard a volley of distant rifle shots from the direction of the south pass, but couldn't be sure in the midst of the gunshots, echoes, and yells from the outlaws below.

Jimmy's .38-40 cracked again, then the barely audible pop of the .22 rimfire in Meg's hands.

The battle at the basin rim settled into a grim war of nerves and scant targets, punctuated occasionally by volleys of gunfire from below. Gun smoke billowed from dozens of spots along the sides of the pass. Quick flashes of movement and color told Slocum the outlaws were rapidly working their way uphill. And the slugs were steadily climbing upslope as the shooters neared.

Slocum downed one man who made the mistake of showing himself, then set the Peabody aside and picked up his .44-40 Winchester. This fight was going to be close-range work in just a few minutes—

The solid blow against his left arm knocked his hand from the forestock of the Winchester a heartbeat before he heard the flat blast of the pistol shot behind him. An instant of dull numbness, then a searing pain shot through his shoulder and arm. There was no feeling in the fingers of his left hand; he couldn't will them to move. He dropped the Winchester, rolled onto his back, his right hand slashing toward the Peacemaker—and knew he was going to be too late.

A small, wiry man in a straw sombrero already had the bore of a six-gun lined squarely on Slocum's chest. And nobody, not even Slocum, could draw and fire, especially from a prone position, before a man's finger twitched against a trigger. He could only hope the slug didn't hit anything that wouldn't heal.

The shock never came.

Dust puffed from the *vaquero*'s vest and side at the twin muzzle blasts of a handgun and rifle, the distinct blast of Meg's Remington revolver and the sharper crack of Jimmy's .38-40. Then Slocum's Colt was clear of leather, the muzzle swinging into line. He let the hammer slip from beneath his thumb. The Peacemaker bucked. A silver concha on the vest directly above the gunman's heart disappeared under the impact of the slug.

The outlaw dropped his handgun, sank to his knees, and pitched forward on his face, the sombrero crumpled beneath his head.

Slocum drove another round through the crown of the hat, just to make sure the man stayed down. He didn't have time to breathe a sigh of relief. The lip of the pass seemed to explode. Shards of stone, dirt, and gravel formed a dusty haze above them as dozens of rifle slugs raked their positions.

Slocum chanced a quick glance at his left arm, afraid of what he might see. A shattered elbow could cost him the whole arm. He saw no blood. The piercing pain in his arm didn't extend to his hand. The fingers of his left hand wouldn't move.

A slug kicked dirt near Slocum's head, but the shot had come from the side, not downslope. His heart sank. The men from Shiloh had them flanked on both fronts now. It was only a matter of minutes until enough shooters reached the lip of the rim to catch them in a murderous cross fire. Slocum knew they couldn't hold. Not three guns against that many. It was time to get out now, if they still could. Either way, it was going to be close.

Slocum tried and failed to get Jimmy's attention, his hoarse shout muffled by another ragged volley of rifle fire. Jimmy's gaze was turned downslope, Meg's off to her right. Finally, Jimmy cut a quick glance his way. Slocum made a slashing motion with his gun hand, then pointed the Colt back toward the waiting horses. Slocum started to crab back, then heard the rattle of stones beneath boots and horse's hooves behind him.

They weren't going to make it. He had made the field commander's worst mistake. He'd let the enemy get behind him. They were cut off from the horses.

The old Sioux Indian warrior had been wrong, Slocum thought as he cocked the hammer of the Peacemaker. There was no such thing as a good day to die. The tightness in his chest wasn't for himself. It was for two young people who deserved a lot more time on this Earth—

Slocum twisted at the heavy cough of a big-bore shotgun blast nearby, and heard a high-pitched screech of pain. For an instant he thought Jimmy or Meg had been hit, but realized the shrill cry had come from off to the side away from the two young people. A moment later the scuff of boot on gravel behind him reached Slocum's ears. He swung the muzzle of the Colt toward the sound. There was no visible target.

"Steady there, amigo." The baritone voice came from a clump of thick junipers a few feet away. The words carried well over the rattle and echoes of gunfire. "Ease the hammer. The cavalry has arrived."

Slocum didn't lower the hammer right away. The primary rule of survival was to make damn sure there was no trap until you knew who you were up against. "Show yourself."

Juniper limbs scraped against clothing and a tall, rangy man, sun-browned and wearing trail-stained and rough, dusty clothes, stepped into view, a double-barrel shotgun in over-sized hands. The tall man crouched and scuttled to Slocum's side as slugs snarled past overhead.

The man grinned at Slocum, the smile lifting a thick handlebar mustache above startlingly white teeth. "Sergeant Miles Kilgore, Arizona Rangers," the man said by way of introduction. He shouldered the big smoothbore, sent a cloud of buckshot downrange, then glanced back at Slocum as he broke the action and reloaded. "Officially on leave from Nogales, so I'm not really here, along with two dozen of Arizona's best. At the request of the President of Mexico."

Relief washed over Slocum. They might still get killed, but at least they had a better than fighting chance. "I'm Slocum," he said to Kilgore.

"I know. Saw you in action once up in Tombstone." Kilgore paused to blast a buckshot load down the slope. "Saved me the trouble of arresting a couple men. Buried them instead. By the way, General Herrera's compliments, Slocum," he said, ignoring a slug that cut a dime-sized chunk from the brim of his hat. "You held them up here just long enough for everybody to get into position. This fight's about to open for real now.''

''I thought it already had,'' Slocum said.

The words were barely out of Slocum's mouth when the rim of the basin exploded in a thundering belch of muzzle smoke and the blasts of a score or more rifles, handguns, and shotguns. On the timbered slope below, bark chips and pine needles flew from trees. Dust and stone shards kicked loose under the wallop of lead. Startled squawks and cries of pain from the slope rode the echoes of the sudden barrage.

Slocum caught a glimpse of movement below, triggered a snap shot from the Colt, and heard an answering grunt of surprise and pain. Kilgore again cut loose both barrels of his 10-gauge smoothbore, then glanced at Slocum as he reloaded. ''Looks like you got a scratch there. Hit bad?''

Slocum shook his head. ''Don't know. Can't move my fingers. Whole arm's numb.''

''Don't see any serious blood. We'll get a close look at it in a bit.'' Through the haze of dust and powder smoke, Slocum saw a dot of light wink from the far rim of the basin. ''Better grab yourself some dirt, partner,'' Kilgore said grimly. ''It's about to get hotter'n hell up here and even worse down there.''

The ground seemed to shudder beneath Slocum. The familiar rattle of grapeshot raked both sides of the slope below as a brace of cannon thundered off to his left. The piercing squeals of dying horses and screams of injured men followed in the wake of the cannons' throaty thumps.

Slocum peeked through the V-shaped notch of his shooting rest. From the east rim of the basin, a flash and smoke bloomed; a heartbeat later, a sizeable chunk of the quadrangle building exploded in a cloud of adobe dust. That had to be at least a four-pounder to throw that kind of shell, Slocum thought.

''Mexican artillery boys in this bunch are better than most,'' Kilgore yelled above the cannon fire. ''Won't be much left down there when they're done.''

Slocum momentarily forgot the Peacemaker in his hand as the artillery barrage from both basin rims intensified. Over the boom of cannon and blast of exploding shells, Slocum heard the throaty reports of high-powered rifles mingled with the sharper cracks of lighter small arms. Explosive shells, solid ball, and canister rounds hammered the settlement below in a near-constant thunder.

The Confederate flag above the compound spun skyward amid a fog of rock and adobe dust, and fell lazily back into the smoking rubble that had been the front of the quadrangle. Adobe dusted from a wall of the small house in the middle where Meg had been held captive; a bit over a second later, half the building disappeared in a boil of flame, smoke, and dust. Fused explosive shell, Slocum thought idly.

He watched in near detachment as first one, then the other, of Shiloh Dunnigan's powder magazines blew up, adding still more smoke and debris to the scene unfolding below. Moments later, the basin floor was obscured by a dense fog of smoke and dust.

The artillery barrage abruptly stopped. Slocum couldn't be sure how long the village had been pounded by the big guns; when cannon cut loose, minutes seemed like hours before the sudden, deafening silence set in. For a time, Slocum fought the queasy feeling that he was back in the Wilderness or Antietam or Spottsburg or half a dozen other major engagements he'd fought in, a dream-like return to the devastation and carnage of battlefields large and small.

In the abrupt quiet, a call came from downslope: *"No mas! No mas!"* A *vaquero*, hatless and with blood pouring down his face, cautiously stood, hands raised to shoulder height. After a time others, realizing that the man wasn't going to be shot dead where he stood, followed suit.

"Keep a close eye on them, boys!" Kilgore called. "If they so much as fart, shoot them! Hold your positions! We'll gather up prisoners later!" Answering yells came from positions on both sides of the pass. Slocum hadn't even heard the Rangers coming. The Arizona boys were damned good, he mused.

A crackle of small-arms fire from the direction of the south pass, then the rumble of horse's hooves, drew Slocum's attention. "That's Colonel Ortega and the First Lancers, the whole brigade of them," Kilgore said to Slocum. "Tough boys. They'll handle anything left down there."

Before the distant horsemen entered the dust and smoke fog in the basin, Slocum saw a familiar figure on a massive bay stallion. At first he thought it was Don Viejo, but a closer look showed the rider to be younger, more solidly built. The Don's eldest son, handgun drawn, rode beside a slight man in the uniform of a Mexican army colonel. Two score or more of Don Viejo's *vaqueros* flanked the seemingly endless ranks of smartly uniformed Mexican lancers, who soon were swallowed in the battle haze below.

"Well, friend," Kilgore said to Slocum, "looks like it's all over but the mop-up detail. We've got a few minutes. Let's take a look at that scratch of yours."

By the time the Arizona Ranger helped him strip down his shirt, Jimmy and Meg—their faces streaked with sweat, dirt, and powder smudges—were at Slocum's side. Slocum noted that Meg still walked with a distinct limp.

Slocum said worriedly, "Are you two all right?"

Jimmy squeezed his sister's hand. "Back together again. And that's all that matters. Meg felt somethin' pop in her foot on the way up the trail, but neither of us got hit."

"The Lord was watching over us," Meg said softly, "along with some good friends."

"Reckon we're both a little tired," Jimmy said, "but me, I ain't felt better in many a month."

"Sergeant Kilgore, meet Jimmy and Meg Forrest. Two of the best partners a man ever rode with," Slocum said.

Kilgore shook hands with Jimmy and nodded politely to Meg. "I don't know how the four of you did it," he said in open admiration, "but if you hadn't caused so much hell around here, we'd never have been able to get in position to put an end to Shiloh Dunnigan's army."

"*Four* of us?" Slocum asked, puzzled. He saw his own confusion mirrored in Jimmy's eyes.

"I'll tell you both about it later," Meg said hurriedly. She knelt at Slocum's side, lifting his elbow in a small but surprisingly strong hand. "No blood. The skin isn't even broken. It looks like just a bad bruise."

Kilgore grunted his agreement, then leaned forward to pluck something from the dirt. "You're a lucky man, Slocum," the Arizonan said. He held a flattened piece of lead between a thick thumb and forefinger, then pointed at a bright smear on the boulder where Slocum had crouched. "Small-bore handgun. Likely a piddling .32 rimfire. Slug hit the rock, squashed itself flat, ricocheted, and whacked your elbow right where the nerves are most tender. Can you move your hand?"

Slocum tried and winced. "Not yet. No feeling at all."

"You'll know in a few hours whether any nerves are damaged permanently," Kilgore said. "I'll rig a sling for that arm until you know for sure."

"I'll take over here, Sergeant," Meg said. "You have other things to do, I expect."

Kilgore nodded. "Might as well put the six-gun away, Slocum. It's all over here."

"Not quite," Slocum said, his tone cold and tight. "There's still one man down there I want. Dirk Dunnigan. I'm going after him."

"Shiloh? Figured he'd be blown to little bits down in the town, or shot to pieces somewhere along the line."

"He wasn't. I'll lay odds he's still alive, Sergeant, and I know exactly where he is."

Kilgore frowned. "I'll get half a dozen men and we'll go get the bastard." He glanced at Meg. "Sorry about the language, miss."

"I've heard worse, Sergeant," Meg said calmly. "When speaking of Shiloh Dunnigan, 'bastard' is a compliment." Her hand touched the butt of the old .46 rimfire Remington lying beside her. "I'd like nothing more than to kill the dirty son of a bitch myself."

"Me too, Sissy," Jimmy said tightly, "but I gave Slocum my word. Dunnigan's his. It's part of the deal we cut when Slocum agreed to help me find you."

Kilgore glanced from one to the other, thick brows knitted. "I don't know what's going on here, but I'll assume it isn't my business. Slocum, you sure you won't need some help? Provided Dunnigan's still alive?"

"No, Sergeant. This is between him and me. If I'm not back in an hour, you and your men can have him."

"Whatever shines your boots," Kilgore said with a casual shrug. "I'll tell my boys not to shoot you. Watch yourself, Slocum. Likely there's still some more of them alive down there. Better get my men organized. We've got prisoners to guard." The Arizonan strode away, long legs silently carrying his lanky form at a quick clip.

Slocum fumbled with one hand to reload the spent chambers of the Peacemaker. When he stood, he realized the sling that now held his left arm against his chest could be a bit of a hindrance to a cross-draw. But not that much.

Jimmy said, "Slocum, by my count, there ain't but two of 'em left. Shiloh's yours. Brazos is mine."

Slocum nodded. "That was the deal."

"Jimmy, wait," Meg interrupted, alarm in her tone. "There's something I've got to tell you about him. About Brazos . . ."

The voices rapidly faded as Slocum made his way cautiously down the slope. It wasn't easy going. The mountainside had been rough enough to begin with; after the artillery and rifle fire, fallen limbs, twigs, and whole trees littered the few open spaces. Here and there, shells had felled trees as thick as a man's waist. Explosive charges had downed larger trees and laced the trunks of those still standing with shards of shrapnel from iron shell casings. But the stand of pines now just a few yards away seemed to have escaped any direct hits.

As he stalked, Slocum heard the occasional shot from the basin below, the distant shouts of men, the screams of wounded, orders barked by officers. He paused to listen for sounds of danger, heard nothing out of the ordinary following a pitched battle, and glanced toward the floor of the basin.

Smoke and dust still swirled and eddied, but the freshening breeze had cleared away some of the pall. From what glimpses he caught, the settlement called Shiloh looked to be in ruins. Bodies littered the valley, singly and in dark clumps. Once, he saw a knot of men, arms raised, surrounded by uniformed soldiers.

The snake was done for.

All that remained was to cut off the head.

Slocum resumed his silent stalk. The carcass of Dunnigan's horse was only a few yards to his right now. Slocum knew the man was close. He could all but feel Shiloh Dunnigan's presence.

A faint whimper brought Slocum up short. He cocked his head, listening. A distant rifle shot momentarily covered the soft, mewing sounds, like a frightened baby whining for its mother. The whimpers came from behind a deadfall of heavy timber twenty feet away.

Slocum stepped around the edge of the deadfall and stopped.

Dirk Dunnigan lay behind crossed tree trunks, curled into a ball, his knees drawn up against his chest, head down and arms crossed over his neck.

"Dunnigan," Slocum said softly.

There was no response from the huddled form.

Slocum stepped forward and rammed a boot toe into ribs, drawing another whimper. "Stand up, damn you. Or so help me, God, I'll put a slug through a kidney. It's a hard way to die."

Dunnigan's head slowly lifted. The wiry outlaw's chin quivered. Tears of pure terror dampened cheeks smeared with dirt and fallen pine needles.

"Who—are you?" The voice was reedy and quavered.

"As far as you're concerned, I'm the ghost of the soldiers you butchered at Shiloh. Stand up, Dunnigan. Let's see if you're as tough a soldier when you're facing somebody as you are when you shoot them in the back."

Dunnigan blinked his eyes for a moment, as if climbing from sleep—or back from another world. His gaze finally cleared, settling on the sling supporting Slocum's left arm. His chin still quivered. He straightened to a sitting position and lifted his hands.

"I—it's over. Everything I ever worked for—"

"It's not over, Dunnigan. Not as long as you're still breathing. On your feet." Slocum's gaze flicked over the small man's body, noting the Smith & Wesson .44 Russian revolver in the cutaway holster at his hip. "You're armed. I'll give you a chance, Corporal Dunnigan. More of a chance than you gave those prisoners at Shiloh.''

''You can't—'' Dunnigan lifted his hands. ''I surrender. I'm entitled to—treatment as—prisoner of war.''

''So were the unarmed men you killed in cold blood. It's vengeance time, Dunnigan.''

Dunnigan's eyes narrowed. ''You don't talk—like a Yankee.''

''I'm not. I'm from Georgia. I wore the gray.''

An expression that might have been relief flooded Dunnigan's bloodshot eyes. ''Then we—were on the same side. You know I'm a war hero.''

Slocum shook his head. ''No, we weren't on the same side, Shiloh. And you're not a hero. You not only disgraced the Confederacy but two of those Union prisoners you killed were good friends of mine. A third was a cousin. All of them might as well have been blood kin to me. Now it's time to settle accounts. Pull your side arm, Corporal Dunnigan.''

''You—you'll kill me if I do.''

''I'll kill you either way, Dunnigan. With or without a gun in your hand. I have no use for cowards and backshooters and men who steal from the dead. It's your choice.''

Dunnigan's gaze settled again on the sling around Slocum's arm. ''Wouldn't be fair, you being crippled and all.'' His words seemed to gain some strength; cunning flickered in his eyes.

The dumb bastard actually thinks he's got an edge, Slocum thought. He shrugged. ''I'll take my chances. You see, Dunnigan, I'm not turning my back on you.''

Dunnigan made his move.

Slocum waited a heartbeat as Dunnigan yanked at the grips of the Smith & Wesson. The handgun was a third clear of leather before Slocum's right hand whipped across his body, his knees flexed, and the Peacemaker recoiled against his palm. The slug took Dunnigan just to the left of the breastbone below the rib cage.

Dunnigan staggered under the impact of the 200-grain soft lead slug fired from less than ten feet away; his eyes went wide in disbelief. He looked down at the hole in his shirt, already ringed with blood, the Smith & Wesson forgotten in his hand. He looked up. A drop of blood trickled from the corner of his mouth. His legs buckled. He dropped to his knees.

"Who—are—you?"

"Like I said. A ghost from the past. Adios, Corporal Dunnigan, and good riddance." Slocum shot Dunnigan in the forehead. The impact flung Dunnigan's body backward, draped across a fallen tree trunk.

Slocum stood for a moment, staring at the body and letting the accumulated hate of years seep from him. He holstered the .44-40 handgun—and started, then spun, at the sound of the voice from close behind:

"Just having one arm doesn't slow you down, Slocum. Fast as you were back in Arizona, best I recall." Sergeant Kilgore stepped from behind a tree.

"I thought I told you I didn't need any help," Slocum snapped.

"Believed you. Howsomever, there was still this teeny little chance Dunnigan might have gotten past you. I didn't want that. Besides, now you don't have to cart the carcass someplace far off to prove who you shot. I'll sign the papers vouching for the reward due you on Dunnigan."

Slocum slowly relaxed. "Sergeant, you shouldn't sneak up on a man like that," he said with a half smile. "I could have shot you by mistake."

"Why do you think I stayed behind that tree? My mama didn't raise any fools." Kilgore reached into a shirt pocket and pulled out a couple of thin cigars. "I could use a smoke. How about you, Slocum?" A single pistol shot sounded in the distance; then a deathly quiet settled over the basin.

"If you had just one left, I'd have to kill you for it," Slocum said. He waited as Kilgore scratched a lucifer on a boot heel and lit both their cigars. The smoke was heavy and rich in Slocum's lungs.

"Might as well have a setdown, Slocum," the Arizonan said. "Nothing much else we can do around here." He plopped his butt onto the tree trunk beside the backward-bent body of Shiloh Dunnigan.

Slocum followed suit. For a moment, the two smoked in silence. Finally, Slocum spoke. "What's next, Sergeant?"

"For the boys and me, lend a hand rounding up any strays for a day, two at most. Help out wherever we can. Then a long ride back to Nogales. You?"

Slocum sighed. "I hadn't given it much thought," he said.

12

Slocum leaned back in the overstuffed leather chair in Don Viejo's combination office and library. The itch of restlessness was worse today.

He wasn't wearing out his welcome. His welcome was wearing *him* out.

Don Viejo was the perfect host, except for one small problem. He and his aggravatingly efficient servants—even though the word "servant" didn't fit, exactly; they seemed more like part of the Don's family—wouldn't let Slocum do a damned thing.

The horses were well groomed and freshly shod, a worn cinch replaced on his saddle, the frayed straps of the pack rig replaced. He couldn't even pour his own drinks or light his own smokes; when he had the urge for either, a brown hand always appeared and did it for him. But then, when the brown hand belonged to Pensativa Montalvo, Slocum didn't resent the intrusion a bit.

Every morning a hot bath awaited his return from breakfast. His razor was stropped daily, the clothes he had worn yesterday washed, ironed, neatly folded at the end of the oversized bed in his oversized guest room, his boots freshly polished.

And for the first time in his life, Slocum had to let someone else clean his weapons. He hadn't appreciated how handy a left hand was until it quit working. The Don's armorer, a wiry man getting on in years, damn sure knew a mainspring from a forestock. Slocum couldn't have done a better job himself, even with both hands.

Sitting around doing nothing was slowly driving Slocum around the bend. So he had taken to hiding out in the Don's study during the day. At least there he could escape the swift efficiency of the rancho's house staff, even scratch his butt without being afraid someone would do it for him.

It was time to be moving on. But he couldn't, at least for a few more days. Not until Jimmy and Meg were ready to go. Slocum hadn't brought Jimmy this far and helped him find his sister, only to leave them to fend for themselves and be short a guide and gun on the long ride through hostile country back to the States.

In the first few days after the fight at Shiloh, Slocum had worried over Meg.

He soon realized that his fretting was a wasted effort. Beneath the trim young woman's exterior, Meg was as tough as her brother. Maybe tougher, considering what she had been through. She might have a few nightmares, but she'd make it. Like Jimmy, she was a survivor. A damn pretty survivor, with golden hair, high, firm breasts, and trim legs.

Slocum understood why Scar would have parted with a hefty load of silver for Meg. Different times, different places, different circumstances, Slocum would have laid out a cartwheel or two himself for a night with her. Not now. She had come to trust Slocum, to bare her feelings and fears, her vulnerabilities along with her strengths. He wouldn't betray that trust, especially given what she'd been through at the hands of Shiloh Dunnigan and his bunch.

The torn muscle in Meg's instep was healing nicely. She hardly limped on the foot now. Best of all, the regimental physician from the Mexican army had examined her and pronounced her free of any disease. She no longer felt the little wriggly things crawling inside her.

Slocum sipped at the fine Tennessee bourbon from the Don's impressive selection in the hand-carved walnut cabinet behind the desk. One of the Don's slim cigarillos sent its aromatic trickle of smoke upward from the cut-glass ashtray on the table beside Slocum's chair.

He had everything he needed. And felt totally useless.

Don Viejo and his two tall, handsome sons—mirror images of the father as a younger man, Slocum suspected—were off on horseback somewhere. A ranch the size of the Don's didn't run itself. The elder Viejo could have just told his sons or his *segundo* what needed to be done and stayed in the comfort of this room. Most rich and powerful men would. Not Don Viejo. He enjoyed being in the saddle, doing ordinary *vaquero* work, getting dirty and sweaty along with everyone else. The Don found more pleasure in a new foal than in a sack of shiny gold. Slocum doubted the Don even knew—or cared—how much money he had.

Slocum wanted to go along with them today, but the Don politely suggested he stay behind until his arm had healed itself. Slocum didn't argue. His left elbow was still sore to the touch. And as seemed the case with every tender bruise a man collected, it managed to bump against anything and everything it could reach. But he had almost a full range of motion in his left arm and hand now. The nerves had been bruised but not permanently damaged. It could have been a lot worse. As Kilgore had said, Slocum mused, he *was* a lucky son of a bitch.

That didn't ease the tension of boredom.

Almost two weeks had passed since the showdown at the outlaw stronghold called Shiloh. That had been a good day's work. If you weren't looking at it from the outlaws' viewpoint.

When the battle ended, little more than two dozen of Dunnigan's men were left alive. They were now on their way to Mexico City under heavy guard, to be tried,—and most likely shot,—as traitors.

Almost two hundred of Dunnigan's men—the core cadre of his planned army—died on the basin floor or on the slopes of the mountains. The town itself lay in ruins, reduced to rubble by Mexican cannoneers. It would be rebuilt at General Herrera's orders and returned to the farmers and fruit growers and sheepmen from whom Dunnigan had taken it in the first place.

Thanks to the effectiveness of the Mexican artillerymen, casualties had been light among the attacking force. Kilgore's losses were one Arizona Ranger dead, two others slightly wounded. Of Don Viejo's tough *vaqueros,* two had been killed, four wounded. The Mexican lancers had lost six cavalrymen, with another dozen injured, in the close-quarter fighting.

There had been a few civilian casualties.

There always were in a war, especially one involving artillery. Explosive shell and grapeshot didn't distinguish the innocent from the guilty once the charge left the barrel.

At first, Meg had been upset that the woman named Carla, whose breast had been carved away by Dirk Dunnigan's sadistic consort, had been among the innocent victims. Slocum didn't say so to Meg, but he figured Carla was better off. From the way Meg had described her, Carla was obviously insane. With good cause.

Meg's spirits brightened considerably when Colonel Ortega's troops found the wounded Bill Smith, formerly known as Brazos. The problem was, she found him at the same time Jimmy did, on a cot in the surgeon's tent below the south pass.

Smith was looking down the bore of Jimmy's .41 Lightning when Meg stepped between them. She had a hell of a time convincing Jimmy not to pull the trigger. It finally soaked through Jimmy's brain that Meg was telling it straight, that Smith had taken no part in the rapes and killings up on the Republican—and had, in fact, helped save not only her life, but possibly Jimmy's and Slocum's as well. Along with the lives of scores of men in the forces that attacked Shiloh.

Meg was with Smith now, and Jimmy seemed to be mellowing quickly toward the lean young outlaw. Almost friendly, once he understood the situation. Slocum could see Jimmy thawing by the day as he came to know Smith better. Meg thawed a lot faster. Slocum could see it in her eyes. The same look was reflected in Smith's. It didn't take a genius to tell where that relationship was headed.

The slug Smith had taken in the upper hip had cut no major blood vessels or organs. Smith's hipbone might have been cracked, but not broken. The Mexican army, contrary to popular belief north of the Rio Grande, had some top-flight physicians and surgeons among its ranks. There was no sign of infection. Smith was a strong, healthy young man. In a few days, Smith would once more be able to straddle a horse.

Scar wouldn't.

Like Dunnigan, the Apache was no more. Lieutenant Esteban Morales's crack company of veteran Indian fighters, supplemented by half a dozen Mestizo Indian scouts and a handful of Don Viejo's *vaqueros,* had set a magnificent ambush south of Shiloh. Of the renegades, less than a dozen escaped. Morales had had scar decapitated and the head impaled on a stake to mark the spot where more than eighty Apaches had died. The head, and later the bare skull, would be a reminder to others that all was not whiskey, women, and loot on the renegade trail.

Morales had taken no prisoners.

All told, the haul was impressive. The final tally showed nearly a thousand rifles captured or destroyed, along with half again that many handguns and thousands of rounds of ammunition, from Dunnigan's stronghold. That didn't count the horses or almost fifty thousand dollars in gold and silver in Dunnigan's safe that would have been a good start toward outfitting a sizable army.

There were hardly enough of the outlaws and renegade Apaches left for a decent poker game, let alone a wholesale invasion of the western United States and Mexico.

Best of all, the cooperative—if unofficial—venture between the Mexican and American governments assured there would be no war between the two nations unless the politicians totally screwed things up.

It also had been a profitable venture for Slocum. The five-hundred-dollar reward on Dunnigan would be waiting for him at the Arizona Ranger headquarters in Nogales. With another five hundred dollars in silver from a grateful Mexican president already in his pockets, Slocum was a rich man by frontier standards.

Half the reward on Dunnigan was Jimmy's, if Slocum could convince him to take it. James Daniel Forrest also had a five-hundred-dollar bonus in Mexican coin with which the kid and his sister—and Bill Smith too, Slocum figured—could begin a new life somewhere.

Slocum fussed at himself silently. He had to stop thinking of Jimmy as a kid. The boy had fleshed out, grown up, earned his spurs in the time they'd ridden together. Jimmy was a man now. Might as well get used to the idea.

Slocum had just finished his drink when the door whispered open and Pensativa Montalvo strode into the room, her smile flashing white teeth against dark skin.

Pensativa, Slocum thought, didn't exactly fit her name. There was nothing pensive about her. He didn't know how she always seemed to appear just as he was about to do something for himself over the last few days. In fact, he found himself hoping she would appear.

Just looking at her was enough to ease the monotony.

Pensativa Montalvo, three years a widow, might have been a servant in a household run with less mutual respect between employer and employee. Her primary job seemed to be that of head housekeeper, social-event organizer, and hostess for the widowed Don, whose visitors often included the rich and powerful from both sides of the border. Pensativa filled the latter role well. Just her smile would brighten any social gathering, take the edge off even an angry man. The rest of her wasn't hard to look at either, Slocum conceded.

She was in her early thirties, or so Slocum guessed, tall and voluptuously built, and she carried herself with a grace and pride that bore no touch of haughtiness. Dark brown, almost liquid eyes were set wide above high cheekbones in her oval face, and seemed to draw a man into her soul. She was a gentle sort, but with a sultry smokiness Slocum often had seen in women of Spanish blood. Thick, dark hair fell in soft waves about her shoulders, bared now in the scooped neckline of a simple peasant blouse of pale blue silk. A yellow sash around her trim waist emphasized the flare of hips beneath a long, full skirt that frequently flashed trim, delicate ankles and the high-arched insteps of dainty feet.

Pensativa glanced at Slocum's glass. "Another, Señor Slocum?" Her voice was low, almost husky; she spoke with the musical cadence of Central Mexico rather than border Spanish.

He shook his head. "No, thank you, Pensativa," he said in her native tongue. Pensativa's command of English was quite good, but Slocum was comfortable with Spanish.

She studied his face for a moment, her full lips pursed, a touch of concern in soft brown eyes. "You seem troubled, Señor. Have we done something to offend you during your stay?"

"Not at all. I'm just restless," Slocum said with a smile of reassurance. "I'm not used to being cooped up indoors for so long, even in such gracious company."

The concern faded from her eyes. "And how is your arm today?"

"Much better, thank you." Slocum flexed his left hand. All but one of the fingers curled easily against his palm at his will. The little finger still tingled a bit, and didn't quite close. "Another day or two, I'll be as good as new."

"That is good to hear." She hesitated for a moment, an unasked question in those liquid eyes.

"Something on your mind?" Slocum prompted.

"I was just wondering. The sun is not so strong this afternoon. Would you like to go for a ride? Get away from the hacienda for a time? I know a restful place not more than three miles from here. I go there often." She hesitated briefly, then added, "I should enjoy a ride myself."

Slocum inclined his head in a brief bow. "Nothing would please me more, Pensativa."

Her expression brightened. "Good, very good. I shall ask Pedro to saddle your bay and my mare."

Slocum rode relaxed, thinking it odd the saddle should seem more comfortable than the Don's overstuffed chair. The bay, apparently grown as restless as Slocum, stepped out in his smooth fox-trot. Slocum felt the eagerness in the gelding's powerful muscles. He had to keep a firm rein on the bay to prevent the big horse from breaking into a lope.

Slocum began to feel human again for the first time in days.

Pensativa had been right about the weather. The day was as close to perfect as a man could order from nature's menu. The afternoon sunlight felt warm on his body, its heat tempered by a gentle, cooling breeze from the mountains to the northwest.

He glanced at the woman riding beside him, mounted on a fine-boned, gaited sorrel mare. Pensativa rode sidesaddle; she had not changed from the blouse and skirt. The breeze pressed the pale blue cloth of the blouse against her skin, molding it to the contours of full, firm breasts unrestrained by a corset.

Slocum tried to ignore the tingling pressure at his crotch. Pensativa was a beautiful, sultry woman, and it had been a long time since Jacksboro and Hanna Einreich's bed. He reminded himself that he was a guest, and that he also didn't want to offend Pensativa. Still, almost from that first meeting in the Don's house, he had caught glimpses of her studying him with obvious interest. And unless he read the look in her eyes wrong, maybe more than just passing interest. He knew she was aware of the appreciative looks he had turned her way. A man would have to be gelded not to appreciate a woman like Pensativa.

They didn't talk much during the ride, each content to simply enjoy the day and the feel of a horse beneath them.

The three miles slipped by quickly.

Pensativa's private place, as she called it, proved to be as comfortable as the ride. Sunlight filtered through cottonwood and chinaberry trees, dappling the small clearing surrounded by lush green grass and bisected by a stream barely a yard wide. The soft gurgle of flowing water over smooth stones mingled with the calls of birds and rustle of breeze through the trees.

They sat side by side, shoulders almost touching, on the blanket Pensativa had brought—along with a bottle of the Don's best tequila—and listened to the comforting sounds of their hobbled horses cropping the rich grass.

After a time, Slocum felt her hand settle gently on his forearm. Her fingers were cool, a sign of the nervousness he had sensed in her when they reined in beneath the trees.

"You will be leaving soon, Slocum?" she asked. At least he had been able to convince her not to call him "Señor" during the ride.

"Yes, soon." The touch of her hand on his arm seemed to flow through and warm Slocum's body.

She sighed deeply. The motion lifted her breasts; they were neither overly large nor small, but perfectly shaped, the erect buds of her nipples and their quarter-sized dark rings clearly visible through the thin blue cloth of the peasant blouse. The motion also increased the tightness in Slocum's groin.

"Then I am glad I brought you here." The hint of shyness faded from the sultry brown eyes. "I do not wish you to think of me as a common *puta,* Slocum. But since the first time I saw you, I have been reminded that it has been three long years since I have had a man. It is a brazen thing to say, but—"

Slocum reached over with his semi-working left hand and placed a finger on her lips. "Don't speak of yourself that way, Pensativa," he said softly. "You are anything but a common *puta*. You are a woman with class."

She reached up with her free hand, held Slocum's finger against her lips, and kissed it lightly. Then she turned into his arms and kissed him, her full lips moist and slightly parted. After a moment, she broke the kiss.

"After—so long," she said breathlessly, "perhaps I—have forgotten how to please a man."

Slocum pulled her closer. "I doubt that, Pensativa."

She kissed him again, deeper and more urgently; the tip of her tongue caressed his. She took his left hand in hers and lifted it to her right breast. Her breathing quickened. Slocum gently kneaded the firm but yielding flesh, then let his palm rest on the engorged nipple. He could feel the rapid thump of her heart. She moaned softly, deep in her throat.

Slocum's right hand seemed to move of its own will, down past her ribs, along the outside of her thigh. As his fingers eased beneath the folds of her peasant skirt, she instinctively spread her knees. She dropped a hand to the swelling at his crotch.

The skin of her thigh was warm, smooth, and firm to the touch. Slocum's fingers inched slowly higher until they touched the dense thatch between her legs. The heat and moisture there, along with the musky scent of aroused woman, threatened to overload Slocum's nervous system.

"A—moment—please," she said.

She stood and stripped the peasant blouse over her head, the dappled sunlight dancing over perfectly formed breasts. The riding boots came off, the skirt came down, and she stood naked before him, long muscular legs joined at the thick triangle of black hair on full hips. She looked like a carved statue of a dusky goddess, Slocum thought. Her breasts rose and fell rapidly with her breathing.

Slocum stripped as Pensativa spread the blanket they had been sitting on. She stretched out, legs slightly spread, and reached for him. Her skin was almost hot to the touch as he came to her, a thin sheen of sweat already forming where their bodies touched.

"Please—Slocum—wait," she gasped. "Your arm—" She rolled over, pulling him with her, until she was on top, her damp crotch pressed against his. "Now—please—"

Slocum stalled a bit. His tongue worked against her lips and throat; he had to bend his neck forward only slightly to take first one, then the other, of the erect brown nipples between his lips. At the same time, he slipped his right hand between the her thighs. His fingers parted the damp folds of her labia, and his index finger stroked the bud of her clitoris.

She reached back, moaning softly, and guided his shaft into her. He entered her slowly and carefully; despite the copious flow of her juices, she was surprisingly tight. The moist heat worked its way down Slocum's shaft. Her internal muscles flexed; her breath caught in her throat for a moment as the full length of Slocum's shaft buried into her. For several heartbeats, neither of them moved, savoring the rich, full warmth.

After a moment she moaned again, then leaned her shoulders back, her knees almost in Slocum's armpits as she straightened her body. The movement drove him even deeper into her. Slocum fought back the natural urge to start moving his hips, letting her set the pace and take the lead. Her head was thrown back, lips parted, eyes closed, hair falling almost to the dark round pigment surrounding her nipples. Slocum stroked both her breasts, the fingers of each hand toying with her taut nipples.

She began to move, slowly at first, hips lifting only slightly, then settling back down. A soft whimper formed in her throat. The movement of her hips increased until her tight wetness stroked almost the entire length of Slocum's shaft.

A few moments later she cried out softly, shuddered, convulsed; the tight pulsations of her vaginal muscles, the sharp gasps from her throat almost caused Slocum to lose control. He barely managed to hold back the urgent swelling and growing pressure in his testicles.

His patience was rewarded only moments later when she convulsed again, her crotch thrust hard against his, their pelvic hairs pressed together, growing wetter. Slocum could hold back no longer. The pressure surged upward from his balls, his shaft swelled even more, and then the almost-painful spasm of pleasure wracked his body as his throbbing shaft expelled fluid into her, triggering gasps from them both. Her muscles rippled against his shaft, milking the final drops from him; the orgasm seemed to last a long time before the pulsing of Slocum's shaft slowed.

Pensativa collapsed onto his chest, her breathing still shallow and rapid. Through the sweat of two bodies, Slocum felt the sticky ooze from the lips of her vagina against the curly black hair at his crotch.

For several minutes, neither of them spoke. Slocum felt his shaft begin to soften. Then Pensativa pushed herself up on her elbows and smiled down through waves of dark hair at Slocum.

"My God," she whispered, her voice husky, "I had forgotten such—such feelings, such pleasure." Her smile turned into a bit of a lecherous leer. "And I do not believe I am yet finished with you, Slocum."

He sighed, aware that he was about to go completely limp inside her. "I'm afraid I may be out of action for a while, Pensativa. I think we've killed it."

"Perhaps." The muscles of her vagina clenched against him, relaxed, clenched again, massaging his shaft. She wasn't as tight now, and she was wetter than ever, their mingled juices flooding out of her. But Slocum's wilting stopped. His shaft began to swell again. "And perhaps not," Pensativa said.

Their lovemaking was slower and less urgent this time, more gentle, but when the peak came it was even sharper and more intense than before. Slocum held Pensativa close as their breathing slowly returned to normal. She made no effort to revive him.

Finally, she rolled onto her side and smiled at him. "Thank you, Slocum."

"The pleasure was all mine, Pensativa."

She giggled like a schoolgirl. "Was not."

"Was too."

"Was not."

"There is a way to settle this argument," she said, her eyes twinkling in mischief, "but I would have to come to your room tonight. If you have no objection."

Slocum pulled her to him. "Anyone who would object to such an offer would be either a gelding or a complete idiot," he said. "But on a more serious note, I not only wouldn't object—I'd be honored."

"You are no idiot," she said with a deliciously wicked grin, "and you are certainly no gelding. And the honor would be all mine."

"Would not."

"Would too."

"We're up to two nights now," Pensativa said. "Perhaps it will take more to settle this argument. . . ."

Slocum checked the hitches on the two pack animals a final time, then turned to Don Viejo.

Pensativa stood at the Don's side, flanked by a small group of *vaqueros* and household staff. Slocum smiled at Pensativa. She smiled back. They had said their good-byes last night. Slocum's knees were still weak from the extended farewell.

Don Viejo extended a hand. "You are welcome to stay in my poor *jacale* as long as you wish, my friend," he said.

Slocum took the hand. "We've imposed on your hospitality longer than we should, Don Viejo. It's time we moved on."

The aging rancher nodded. Like Slocum, he didn't care for extended good-byes. The longer they dragged on, the greater the chance of embarrassment, of the outward show of inner emotion. "May God ride with you, Slocum."

"And you, Don Viejo. Thank you—" he shifted his glance to Pensativa—"and your people, who made our stay here so enjoyable."

Pensativa nodded, a twinkle of mischief in the dark eyes. "The pleasure was all ours, Señor Slocum," she said.

Slocum had to grin at their private joke. The running debate over whose pleasure it really was had been going on for several nights. It wasn't settled yet.

Don Viejo gave no outward sign of knowing what went on between Pensativa and Slocum. Slocum knew better. He also knew if the Don had any objections, he would have told Slocum as much.

"Should you come this way again, Slocum, be sure to stop by," Don Viejo said. "The door is never barred to you and your friends."

"I'll make it a point, my friend," Slocum said. He toed the stirrup, mounted his bay, and glanced at the trio already in the saddle.

Jimmy forked the tight-twisted, antsy little sorrel he'd ridden since the run-in with the two unknown dead men up in the Beaver River country. It seemed to Slocum that Jimmy had grown two inches in the last month.

Meg, dressed in men's clothing for the trail, her head carried high and proud beneath the flat-crowned leather Plainsman-style hat, waited at Bill Smith's side. The young man known as Brazos in a former life seemed a bit pale, and carried more of his weight in one stirrup than the other. The hip still bothered him, Slocum knew, but less by the day. And he never complained. If they took it slow and easy on the trail, Smith would be fully mended by the time they reached Nogales.

Slocum planned to take it easy anyway. Thanks to Pensativa, he was a tad behind in his sleep. A slight smile touched his lips as he wondered how a man could be so completely and thoroughly relaxed and at peace, but so totally worn down at the same time. He pushed the thought aside.

"All set, folks?" Slocum asked.

"Ready when you are, Boss," Meg said with a smile that brightened an already pleasant, sun-washed day.

"Might as well move out then," Slocum said. "It's a long ride to Nogales." He kneed the bay into motion north by northwest. As he rode past Pensativa, he touched his fingers to his hat brim and silently mouthed: "Was not."

"Was too," she mouthed back.

Slocum chuckled to himself. He was still grinning like a schoolkid when the buildings of Don Viejo's ranch grew small in the distance.

Nogales was an outwardly sleepy border town, with a handful of Anglo faces among the mostly Mexican population, but it was hospitable enough. Slocum had briefly considered wintering here; it was mid-September, and the high mountain passes would be snowed under.

When he first realized what the season was, it surprised him a bit. It didn't seem possible that almost three months had passed since James Daniel Forrest had stuck a pipsqueak .22 rifle muzzle in his ear. But it had been three months well spent.

And it hadn't been boring.

The mountain snows didn't mean that much anyway. Jackson Hole and the Grand Tetons would still be there come spring. Slocum hadn't had any particular reason to go there, except that he liked the place.

He leaned against the adobe wall of the stage station, mouthing a match stem sharpened into a toothpick, idly waiting for the Nogales-to-Tucson stage. He wouldn't be on it, but Jimmy, Meg, and Bill Smith would.

Slocum was pleased he had set such an easy pace on the long ride from deep in Mexico. Smith's hip had healed, but more importantly, Slocum had gotten to know Smith—and Meg—a lot better on the way.

Smith wasn't a bad sort. Not really an outlaw; he didn't have a mean streak in him. Once Slocum heard Smith's story, he understood how a confused young man might wind up in an outlaw gang. Everybody made at least one mistake sometime during his life.

On the trail to Nogales, Slocum also had seen the deepening of feeling between Meg and Smith, a bond that went beyond shared pain. Considering what they'd both been through, it would take some time, but he had no doubt they'd be able to put the past behind them and share a marriage bed.

Jimmy had warmed to Smith more by the day too. They seemed more like brothers now. A fresh start in California would be good for all three of them.

They'd also learned a bit about Slocum's past. Confederate sharpshooter, a sniper both feared and respected by his counterparts in blue—and their officers. The only one of his clan to survive the war years and return to the family farm in Georgia with the intent to forever hang up his guns.

It hadn't worked out that way.

When the carpetbagger judge and the hired gun who passed himself off as a lawman tried to take over the farm with a damn lie that the taxes hadn't been paid, Slocum unpacked his handguns. He killed them both, burned the house, barn, and crops, saddled up, and headed west. He'd been drifting ever since.

All told, he conceded, it hadn't been such a bad life. He had been places, done things, met people of all races, cultures, and standards of morality, been flat broke at times and flush at others. He was his own boss. He went where he wanted, even if he didn't know where that might be at the precise time he toed the stirrup.

Meg stepped through the station door, interrupting Slocum's musings, and put a hand on his arm.

"Slocum," she said softly, "I can never repay you for what you've done. For Jimmy, for me—and for Bill."

He smiled his reassurance. "No repayment necessary. Just find a nice place in California and have yourself a good life."

"Do you come to California?"

"Sometimes."

"Will you find us—and visit—when you do?"

Slocum nodded. "Bet on it." In the distance, a rooster tail of dust rose behind the speck that was the approaching stage. "Got your tickets, tack, and tuck?"

"In hand, packed up and waiting," Meg said. "May I ask what your plans are, since you won't go with us?"

Slocum's hand unconsciously brushed the folded message in his hip pocket, the second telegram he'd received in reply to the second one he'd sent. He'd wired Hanna Einreich, on impulse: "Married yet?" The reply had come back. "No. What the hell are you doing in Nogales?" He'd ignored the question and wired. "Busy this winter?" The telegrapher's finger had barely left the key when the reply had come back. "Nope. Come on."

Slocum sighed. "Oh, I might wander back to Jacksboro."

"Tell Dub Packer hello," Jimmy said, stepping from the station. He winked at Slocum. "Hanna too. Looks like our ride's about to get here."

Smith joined them a moment later, three tickets in his hand, clean-shaven, slim, and handsome in his new traveling suit and string tie. As the stage rumbled into view on Nogales's main street, Slocum shook hands all around; it wasn't enough for Meg. She gave him a long, sincere hug and a kiss on the cheek.

Slocum waited until their gear was stowed and Meg and Smith climbed into the stage. Jimmy reached for the door, then hesitated.

"Just remembered, Slocum. I owe you some money."

"Since when?"

"Since up on the Beaver. Remember, I hired you to do a job. You did it." Jimmy reached in his pocket and handed Slocum two gold coins. "I pay my debts. Here's the toughest twenty bucks you've ever made, I'll bet."

Slocum chuckled. "Oh, I don't know about that. You should try going up against the poker players up on the second floor of the White Elephant in Fort Worth sometime. Gets a lot more tense there than it was where we've been." Slocum shook Jimmy's hand again. "Good luck, amigo."

"You too," Jimmy said. He released Slocum's grip, mounted the stage step, and glanced back. "Keep your hair on, Slocum," he said.

Slocum watched as the stage pulled out, then grew smaller behind its dust cloud, a momentary sense of loss tightening his chest.

Then he shook his head, glanced at the sun, and reached in his pocket for a cigarillo. He noticed the small triangular tear on the sleeve of his favorite cotton shirt.

No doubt about it.

He needed a seamstress.

And he could make several miles toward Jacksboro before sundown.

LONGARM

Explore the exciting Old West with one of the men who made it wild!

J. R. ROBERTS
THE GUNSMITH